D0208748

RANDOM
HOUSE
LARGE
PRINT

BOOKS BY ALEXANDER McCALL SMITH
AVAILABLE FROM RANDOM HOUSE LARGE PRINT

IN THE ISABEL DALHOUSIE SERIES

The Sunday Philosophy Club
Friends, Lovers, Chocolate
The Right Attitude to Rain
The Careful Use of Compliments
The Charming Quirks of Others
The Comforts of a Muddy Saturday
The Lost Art of Gratitude
The Uncommon Appeal of Clouds
The Forgotten Affairs of Youth

IN THE NO. 1 LADIES' DETECTIVE AGENCY SERIES

The No. 1 Ladies' Detective Agency
The Full Cupboard of Life
In the Company of Cheerful Ladies
Blue Shoes and Happiness
The Good Husband of Zebra Drive
The Kalahari Typing School for Men
Morality for Beautiful Girls
Tears of the Giraffe

IN THE PORTUGUESE IRREGULAR VERBS SERIES

Portuguese Irregular Verbs
The Finer Points of Sausage Dogs
At the Villa of Reduced Circumstances

IN THE 44 SCOTLAND STREET SERIES

44 Scotland Street
Espresso Tales

The Girl Who Married a Lion and Other Tales from Africa

Trains and Lovers

Trains and Lovers

ALEXANDER McCALL SMITH

RANDOM HOUSE
LARGE PRINT

These are works of fiction. Names, characters, places, and incidents either are the product of the author's imagination or are used fictitiously. Any resemblance to actual persons, living or dead, events, or locales is entirely coincidental.

Published in the United States of America by
Random House Large Print.
In association with Pantheon Books, New York.
Distributed by Random House, Inc., New York.

Originally published in Great Britain by Polygon Books, an imprint of Birlinn Limited, Edinburgh, in 2012.

Excerpts from "Night Mail" and "Heavy Date" by W. H. Auden appear courtesy of Edward Mendelson, Executor of the Estate of W. H. Auden, and Random House, Inc.

Cover design and illustration by Christopher Silas Neal

The Library of Congress has established a Cataloging-in-Publication record for this title.

ISBN: 978-0-8041-2095-1

www.randomhouse.com/largeprint

FIRST LARGE PRINT EDITION

Printed in the United States of America

10 9 8 7 6 5 4 3 2 1

This Large Print edition published in accord with the standards of the N.A.V.H.

This book is for
Christine and Rachel Taylor

Trains and Lovers

1

"I THINK THAT'S A FISHING BOAT."

It was. He saw it from the train, but not for more than a minute or two, as the line followed that bit of coastline only for a short time before it suddenly swerved off, as railway lines will do. The view of the North Sea was lost, and trees closed in; there was the blue of the sea one moment and then the blurred green of foliage rapidly passing the window; there was slanting morning sun, like an intermittent signal flashed through the trees.

THIS IS THE STORY OF FOUR PEOPLE, ALL strangers to one another, who met on that train, and of how love touched their lives, in very different ways. Love is nothing out of the ordinary, even if we think it is; even if we idealise it, celebrate it in poetry, sentimentalise it in coy valentines. Love happens to just about everyone; it is like measles or the diseases of childhood; it is as predictable as the losing of milk teeth, or the breaking of a boy's voice. It may visit us at any time, in our youth but also when we are much older and believe we are beyond its reach; but we are not. It has been described as a toothache, a madness, a divine intoxication—

metaphors that reflect the disturbing effect it has on our lives. It may bring surprise, joy, despair and, occasionally, perfect happiness.

But for each person who is made happy by love, there will be many for whom it turns out to be a cause of regret. That is because it can be so fleeting; one moment it may take our breath away, the next it may leave us bereft. When it does that, love can be like a haunting, staying with us for year after year; we know that it is gone, but somehow we persuade ourselves that it is still there. The heart has more than its fair share of ghosts, and these ghosts may be love, in any of its many forms. I knew one who fell deeply in love at nineteen—smitten, overwhelmed; astonished to find that all he wanted to think about was the other; unbelieving, at first, that this had happened to him. Thirty years later, he found the person he had loved, to whom timidity, if not shame itself, had prevented him from declaring his feelings, regularly coming to him in his dreams. So much had happened in those intervening years, but none of it had been shared, as life had taken them in very different directions. Nobody would choose to be in love like that, to hold on so strongly to something that was no longer there. Yet we admire such instances of tenacity, finding nobility in loss and in the way in which some people bear it.

If it were not for the train journey on that day, these four would never have met. Journeys may be like that, may bring together people who would otherwise never have known of each other's existence. In that respect, long journeys have something in common with military service or boarding school, or even the shared experience of some natural disaster. Such things bring us into contact with people we would never have encountered but for the sharing of danger or unhappiness.

Journeys are not only about places, they are also about people, and it may be the people, rather than the places, that we remember. Those with whom one shares a carriage on the Trans-Siberian Railway may well be remembered, even if the names of the places in which the train stops are soon lost. Of Kirov, Perm, Omsk and Ussuriysk, all of them stops on that long journey, most travellers, other than the locals, will probably remember only Omsk—for its sheer, prosaic finality, and for the fact that of all possible railway stations in the world, we are here in one called Omsk. I know nothing of Omsk, but it seems to me that its name is redolent of ending, a full stop; not a place for honeymoons or rhapsodies. Omsk.

Or Adelstrop. **Yes, I remember Adelstrop, for the train stopped there in the heat**—that is Edward Thomas. The poet was on a train journey into rural Oxfordshire, at a time when there was still an England of quiet villages and hedge-bound fields, and when a train might unexpectedly draw to a halt at a small place and there might be birdsong audible behind the hissing of steam. Nothing happens there, other than the stopping of a train and the escape of pent-up steam, but it brings home how suddenly and surprisingly we may be struck by the beauty of a particular place and moment.

Edward Thomas was not alone in sensing the poetic possibilities of the train. Auden's "Night Mail" is entirely concerned with a rail journey: **This is the Night Mail crossing the border / Bringing the cheque and the postal order.** You can hear the train in those lines; you can feel its rocking motion.

And then there is the poet Kenneth Koch, who while travelling in Kenya came to a railroad crossing at which this sign was posted: **One train may hide another.** This was meant, of course, as a warning to drivers of the fact that the train you see may not be the only train to reckon with, but it also meant, as Koch points out in his poem, that there are many things in this life that conceal other things. One letter may mean another is on the way; one hitch-hiker may deliberately hide another one by the side of the road; offer to carry one bag and you may find there is another one hidden behind it, with the result that you must carry two. And so on through life. Do not count on things coming in ones.

Trains may hide one another, but they may also hide from us what they have in store—the meetings, the disclosures, the exchanged glances, the decisions we make or the insights that strike us on a journey. Trains are everyday, prosaic things, but they can be involved in, be the agents of, so much else, including that part of our human life that for so many far outweighs any other—our need for love—to give it and to receive it in that familiar battle that all of us fight with loneliness.

2

THERE WERE FOUR PEOPLE SITTING TOgether on this train—three men and one woman. One of the men, wearing a corduroy jacket, was somewhere in his late forties, as was the woman seated opposite him. His name was David, and the woman was called Kay. She might have been a bit older—in her fifties, perhaps. David was well-groomed; there was an expensive look to him, as there sometimes is to people who lead sheltered lives, who have always had everything provided for them. The other two were young men, both somewhere in their twenties; one, Andrew, with dark hair and eyes of a rather unusual colour; the other, Hugh, tousle-haired, was well-built—he looked as if he might be good at the playing of a boisterous contact sport.

The journey on which these people met, the journey from Scotland to England, is not a particularly long one—four or five hours, depending on how many stations are stopped at. But four hours is long enough for conversations to develop and for people to reveal to others something of themselves. A friendship may be conceived in four hours; a short book finished and put away; a life remembered.

The train links Edinburgh with London. It leaves Edinburgh behind it and begins its journey over the rich farmland of East Lothian. Then there is a coast, which brings the sight of cliffs and sea-birds; and the North Sea, which was still and smooth that day under the clear morning light. Andrew, seated at the window, looked out and saw a boat ploughing across the field of blue, and he said to the woman seated next to him, the first thing that any of them said that day: "I think that's a fishing boat."

She looked at him, and saw a young man in his mid-twenties, not much more than that, rather slender, but not slight. She noticed his eyes, which were that striking shade of green that some people are blessed with and that in some lights could appear almost grey. She thought that she had once met somebody who looked like him, but she could not remember where or when it was. It was unlikely that it was this particular young man, as she was in Scotland, so far away from home, which was in Perth in Western Australia. And Andrew, from the way he spoke, was Scottish.

"Yes," she said. "A fishing boat." And then she added, "I suppose there are still some fish left. Enough for a few boats here and there."

He nodded and then he looked at her. He was never sure with people who sounded like that. They might be Australian, but they might equally well be New Zealanders, and he had been told that New Zealanders were sensitive about being taken for Australians. He was not sure if it worked the other way round; he could not think of why the big should be put out by being taken for the small. It was easy, of course, to understand how the small might feel that way.

"You're . . . ," he began.

"My name is Kay."

"Andrew."

"I'm from Perth. Not the Perth here in Scotland, but the one in Australia. Our Perth."

He smiled. "The one that's nearer Singapore than it is to Sydney?"

She said, "Yes. We can get to Singapore very quickly. Bali too."

This incipient conversation, still at the level of the sort of small talk that travellers engage in—and rarely get beyond—was listened to by the two others in the group of four seats. David noticed, as had Kay, the colour of the young man's eyes. He looked at them again. He said, "I've been in Singapore."

Andrew turned to look at him. He sounded American, but then he remembered what he had thought about Australians and New Zealanders. Canadians did not like to be taken for Americans; disparity in size, of course—it was the same sensitivity.

So he said, "You must be Canadian."

David shook his head. "American. But close enough, I suppose—at least in my part of the world,

New York State. We're almost in Canada up in Buffalo."

And this was the signal for the other young man, sitting opposite Andrew, to say, "I've always thought that Buffalo is a wonderful name for a place."

"Have you?" said David. "For us, it's just our place. You get used to names, don't you?" This young man, Hugh, who was English, smiled. "I'm sure you do," he said. He paused, and then began, "You've been . . ."

"At a conference," said David. "A conference in Edinburgh. And now I have to go home. A night in London, and then the flight home."

Now Kay turned to Andrew, "Are you going to London?" The train stopped at Newcastle and York, and sometimes stations in between. People went to these places too.

"Yes."

She hesitated. "May I ask why?"

Andrew did not mind the question. "I'm going to start a job."

She waited for him to say more, but he did not. Yet he did not seem to be discouraging her, and so she asked, "What is it?"

"I'll tell you," he said.

3

I DON'T COME FROM ANYWHERE YOU'D KNOW, said Andrew. Just Scotland. Just a place on the west coast, a place called Oban. It's a harbour town. There used to be fishing boats, and I think there are one or two still going out, but nowadays it's mostly ferries. You can go by ferry from Oban to the Hebridean islands—to Colonsay, to Mull, to the islands beyond, places like South Uist and Lewis. There are hills and rivers and sea lochs. It's beautiful, I suppose, but you get used to that and you don't notice it when you live there.

My father was one of the local doctors. He died five years ago, and I miss him a lot, you know. I never thought I would. You take your parents for granted, don't you? My mother remarried after not much more than a year. I found that hard; I know I shouldn't have done, but I did. That's another thing about your parents: you don't want them to have anybody else in their lives. Why should they need that? They have you, don't they? That's the way I thought.

My mother remarried, to a man called Alastair, who owns a company that builds golf courses. Or he owns most of it. He thinks about golf all the time and talks about nothing else. Does she notice it? If she does, then she gives no sign of it and certainly never looks bored. You can always detect boredom, can't you? It's there in the eyes, in that rather glazed, unfocused look. You can always tell; and she never looks like that when Alastair talks about who's playing at St. Andrews or Troon or wherever. I imagine that she's just very grateful that she found somebody else when there are so few men around—or eligible men, I should say. The moment any man becomes available—through divorce or because his wife has died—he'll be snapped up immediately. Women plot that, I think. They have lists of available men and then match-make. Don't smile; it's true, it really is.

Alastair did his best. I don't think he liked me very much—I have absolutely no interest in golf—but he was marrying my mother, after all, and he had to make an effort.

"Andrew," he said. "I want you to know that you are always welcome under my roof. You know that, don't you? It's your home now, and so any time—any time at all—that you want to come and stay for a few days, just do so."

He said **a few days,** and I noticed that. How can a home be your home if it's only for a few days?

My mother had been listening, and understood my response. "Alastair means it, darling," she whispered. "Sometimes he doesn't put it quite as he might. He hasn't got a way with words, as you have."

I nodded, but looked away.

"And I'm sure you can see how important this is for me," she went on. "We don't have many chances of happiness in our lives, you know. One or two, perhaps. And so I could hardly turn down his offer, could I? I know that you might feel a little bit . . . how shall we put it? Possessive?" She looked at me, as if for confirmation of my possessiveness.

She reached out to touch me. "Boys can feel that way about their mothers," she said.

I resolutely avoided her eye. I thought of my father; he would not have liked Alastair. He would not have approved of the golf, nor of the political sentiments he expounded. My father came from a different culture; he had spoken Gaelic as a boy; he believed in equality; he understood what it was to be poor and on the edge of things, as many of his patients were.

"I'm happy for you," I said, forcing out the words.

She sighed. You can't deceive your own mother, I thought. That's the one person, the only one, to whom you will always be transparent.

"Can one try to be happy?" she now said, looking at me with a discomforting intensity. "You're the one who thinks about these things, aren't you? I can't cope with such questions, but it's an interesting one, isn't it? If you have to try to be happy, the seed of happiness simply isn't there. It's like trying to be brave, maybe. You can't be brave if you have to try. Brave people just **are**."

LISTENING TO WHAT ANDREW SAID TO KAY, David thought: Hold on, hold on—you **can** try to be brave, just as you can try to be anything else you decide to be. You can try to be modest; you can try to be tolerant; you can try to be forgiving, when in your heart of hearts you are none of these things. You can be selfish by inclination and yet be generous when the time comes to give; lots of people are like that. They force themselves to be charitable. Look at all those wealthy types who set up charitable foundations when they suddenly realise they're getting old and will not be able to take it with them. Are they being generous, or are they simply **acting** the part? And then he thought: Does it really matter if people think you are something you're not? No, he decided, it did not. We don't owe others a duty of sincerity: Why should we?

ANDREW CONTINUED: THEY WENT AWAY TO get married, to Portugal, to the Algarve, where Alastair had a house beside a golf course. My mother asked me if I wanted to come, and of course

I accepted. But the date they had settled upon was shortly before my university exams, and I would have had to make both the journey out and the return within three days.

"Naturally, we'll understand if it's just too difficult," she said. "These exams of yours are important, aren't they?"

I nodded. We both saw our way out.

"I think perhaps you should stay in Scotland," she said. "It would be awful if there were some problem with the flight home and you missed the exams, wouldn't it?"

I agreed that it would. My relief, I think, was as evident as hers.

"There'll be photographs," she said. "You can imagine that you were there."

"Yes. That's right. Photographs."

In the photographs they were both smiling with what seemed to me to be relief. Both of them had lost their first spouses, and both had obviously experienced what I understand is the strangeness of not having anybody about the house when one has been married for years. Something is missing; something is incomplete. Now they had found one another and their reaction was sheer relief. Normality had been restored.

With an inheritance from my father I had paid the deposit on a flat in Edinburgh. It had three bedrooms and I let these to fellow students, which paid half the mortgage. Alastair offered me help with the repayments, but I declined.

"There's no shame in accepting money," he said. "I did. I accepted a lot, actually."

I wondered who had offered him money, and when this had happened. I looked at him in a new light. This was not a man who had built a golf course with his own resources; this was a man who had accepted a lot of money.

"I can get by," I said. "I've got a part-time job in a coffee bar. I get the rent from the others."

"So you're a **rentier,**" he said, smiling at the jibe. "Just like the rest of us."

I said nothing. He was watching me.

"You know something?" he said at last. "The best advice I can give you: marry money."

I stared at him. "Why?"

"Because money makes money." His tone was patient, as if he were explaining the facts of economic existence to one who knew nothing about them.

"What about love?"

He laughed. "Marriage and love have nothing to do with one another." He seemed pleased with this observation, as if he had just minted a memorable aphorism.

I wanted to ask him: Do you love my mother? Or is the fact that you married her nothing to do with love?

He must have anticipated the objection, as he soon corrected himself. "Perhaps I shouldn't say that. Perhaps not so firmly. There's a sort of love that comes with being married to somebody, but it's different, you know, to the love that makes your heart do a somersault. That's infatuation, or whatever they call it. It's not love."

"So what is this love that comes with being married?"

He shrugged. "Being fond of somebody? Being nice? Wanting them not to go away?"

Wanting them not to go away . . . Alastair was far from poetic, but the line struck me with its poetic force. **I didn't want you to go away** . . . It was certainly powerful, and perhaps it was as good a definition of love as any other. He, of course, did not agree with what I was doing at university. We discussed it only once, and then I changed the subject. You can do that by simply looking at people when they bring something up; you look at them and they know—or should know—that you don't value their opinion on the matter. He saw that, and smiled; he smiled because he thought that he was right and that I knew it, and therefore the moral victory was his. He gave me a look that told me all of that, and more.

"I don't know why you're bothering to study—what is it you're doing?" he said. "History of art? Where exactly does that lead?"

There was a sense in which he was right; studying accountancy or law, or medicine for that matter, leads to a career doing what you've spent time learning at university, but this is not the case with studying the history of art. In another sense, though, he was as wrong about that as he was about so much else. Learning about art led me everywhere, and had I wanted to argue with Alastair I could have told him. In my case it led me out of the narrow world of my life in a small Scottish town and into a world of light and intellectual passion. I suppose I was a bit naïve about it, but it seemed to me that in immersing myself in art history I was becoming a member of a world of connoisseurship and understanding. So while other students might concern themselves with economics or engineering, those of us who were studying art history were somehow above all that. We concerned ourselves with truth and beauty and myth and things of that nature. And if we talked about Giotto and Bernini and Titian, it was with the sense that these were the people with whom we belonged. We **understood**.

Of course we had no idea of how pretentious we were, and now, when I think back, even if only it's a year or two ago, I shudder with embarrassment. But perhaps that's not unusual. Perhaps it's a healthy sign to feel that way on the contemplation of one's earlier self; perhaps not to do so is a sign that one has not developed much self-awareness.

In the back of my mind, of course, was the understanding that it would be very unlikely that I would be able to find a job in the art world. I knew that the odds against doing so were discouraging, but somehow I managed to ignore this knowledge. Something would turn up.

And it did.

4

THEY HAD ALL BEEN LISTENING TO THE young man, but it was Kay who had been listening **and** watching. She had looked at his eyes, and noted their colour. She had wondered how she would describe them if she had been writing a diary, which was something she had been thinking of doing on this trip but had not got round to yet. Already many of the memories of the previous two weeks had faded: the smell of that small hotel in St. Andrews; that mixture of bacon cooking for breakfast and the lavender-scented soap in the bathroom; the air from the sea drifting across the golf course; the aroma of coffee in the coffee bar in South Street. She should have noted them down. She should have said something about all that and the light and the hills with sheep on them like small white stones.

She looked at his hands. She could not help it, but she had always looked at the hands of men and wondered how they had caressed the body of their lover. It was unhealthy, she knew, almost a form of voyeurism, but she could not stop herself. Those hands, she thought, were gentle. They were shy. They would move with hesitation, unsure of themselves.

Would she describe him in her diary as beautiful? Yes, she thought; she would. And how would he describe her? She did not like to think of that. There were twenty years between them, and so she imagined he would not bother to describe her at all. Or was that doing him an injustice? His conversation had been revealing. He had told her about himself and his feelings about his stepfather. He had opened up. Twenty years was nothing.

She waited until he had finished what he was saying. Then she asked: "What turned up?"

IT WAS AN INTERNSHIP, HE SAID. THEY DID not advertise it, but sent out a letter to the head of the department of art history at a number of universities, including Edinburgh. It was for three months, this letter said, and the internship could be held over the summer so as to suit undergraduates who had to get back to their courses in September. The duties were not specified, although the auction house was at pains to point out that interns were given every opportunity to participate in the work of the firm and would not be used as cheap labour.

"You should apply," said one of my lecturers, who, for some reason, liked me. I think it had something to do with the fact that I had read one of his books and had told him I found it interesting. That was true: I had enjoyed it and I think he appreciated that.

I remarked that I thought it unlikely I would be chosen. There would be hundreds of applications and presumably they would take only one or two people. "Everybody wants to work there. Everybody."

He shook his head. "Don't be defeatist."

"I'm not. I'm being realistic."

He pressed me for my reasons, and I told him. "These firms are exclusive. They take people who are a bit . . ."

"A bit what?"

"Well-connected. They know people. I don't know anybody."

He stared at me. "Is that what you think the world is like these days? Is that really what you think?"

I nodded. "I'm from Oban. That's nowhere. People down there won't even know how to pronounce it."

He looked incredulous. "Does that matter? Does it matter if somebody comes from somewhere unpronounceable? And it isn't really unpronounceable."

"Plenty of people put the emphasis in the wrong place," I said. "It happens all the time. They emphasise the second syllable; but it should be the first."

He looked serious now. "What a ridiculous conversation, Andrew. Apply, and, if you don't mind, may I give you a bit of advice? Don't go through life giving up before you've even begun."

I did as he suggested and sent in an application. To my surprise, I was invited for an interview.

"I told you so," said my lecturer.

"I'm still surprised."

There was a hint of a smile. "Well, I know somebody there."

I opened my mouth to say something, but it was one of those situations where you think one thing and another thing comes out.

"It's just an interview," I pointed out.

KAY SMILED. "HE KNEW SOMEBODY?"

"Yes," said Andrew. "Exactly."

She shrugged. "That's the way things are, don't you think? It's human nature. We do things for people we know. Everybody does that."

"But there he was saying the world didn't work that way. That's what he said."

Kay smiled again. "Of course he had to say that. That's the official position. People don't admit to doing things in any other way—not these days—but when you scratch the surface, we haven't really changed very much. Look at the way people try to make points of contact with others when they meet. Look at the way you instinctively try to establish whether somebody you meet for the first time knows somebody you know. Watch people do it. **I'm from such and such a place**. Oh yes? So you know So-and-So? **Yes!** And So-and-So? **No, I don't**

know her, but of course there's So-and-So. That's how it works."

"I suppose so. But why?"

"Because we don't like impersonality. Maybe . . ."

David joined in. "Because we had to."

She asked him: "Had to what?"

"Because we had to co-operate. That's deep in the genes. We had to co-operate with one another and so we needed to know whether the stranger was a threat. Survival—that's what it is. Survival."

I sound like a socio-biologist, he thought, with one of their reductive explanations that made all of life about hunting or mating—scientific ancestor worship, as one of his friends had put it.

She thought about what he had said. Had to co-operate? Not any more? She glanced at Andrew. "And then?"

I'M NOT SURE HOW MANY PEOPLE APPLIED, but it was quite a few. In the end, they took three people that summer. Apart from me, there were two girls, one from the University of Sussex and the other from Oxford. The one from Oxford was called Hermione, and she lived in London. She was tall and very striking-looking. She had that look about her that gave you the impression that she had just had her hair done, and her skin, and her clothes—everything, in fact. She wore jeans that first day, although the letter they had sent us had been very clear on the point. We were not to wear jeans to work.

She noticed that I was looking at her legs and she leaned over and whispered. "They're not jeans. Not really."

"What are they then?"

"They're moleskin. Not from real moles, of course. It's a sort of cotton. Jeans are denim, aren't they?"

I felt somehow privileged that this person seemed to be recruiting me as an ally. "Of course," I said. "I didn't think they were jeans. Well, I did, actually."

"But now you know they're moleskin."

"Yes."

She smiled at me. "They can be a bit stuffy. Even Tommy."

"Who's Tommy?"

She seemed surprised at the question. "Our new boss."

"You call him Tommy?"

She shrugged. "He's my godfather. He's a sweetie."

THE GIRL FROM SUSSEX WAS INTERESTED IN modern art and moved off to work in the department that dealt with that. That left Hermione and me in Old Masters and British Nineteenth Century Art, which was exactly where both of us wanted to be. From her point of view the attraction was the nineteenth century, on which she was writing her second-year dissertation at Oxford; from mine it was partly the period—I was very interested in the seventeenth century at that stage—and partly the fact that I would be working there with Hermione. I had fallen in love, you see. I had fallen in love the moment I saw her; the instant she looked at me; as soon as she had leaned forward and told me that moleskin was different from denim. There's a song somewhere—I forget who sang it—which asks whether you believe in love at first sight and then gives the answer that yes, it happens all the time. Of course it does. In fact, has it ever occurred to people that love at first sight might be the rule rather than the exception? How many people fall in love gradually rather than on the first occasion they meet the other person?

5

THIS QUESTION, POSED ALMOST RHETORICALLY, had a noticeable effect on each of them. Kay frowned, and looked intensely at the young man, as if to coax an answer out of him. But he said nothing, and his question hung in the air. The other young man, Hugh, looked down at the table that separated the seats on one side from those on the other. There was a magazine on this, and he moved it slightly, lining it up against the edge of the table. David allowed his gaze to move out of the window. He caught sight of a boy standing on a river bank; but it was very fleeting, as the train was moving faster and the world outside had speeded up correspondingly.

6

I REMEMBER EXACTLY WHERE I WAS WHEN I admitted to myself that I was in love with Hermione. It was not when I first saw her, even if that was the point at which I fell in love; there is a difference, I think, between falling in love and knowing it. You know it when you surrender to the feeling; you put your hands up and say, "That's it," or something like that. I suppose it must be the same with any of the admissions that one makes. There comes a time when people say, "All right, I'm a crook" or "I admit it, I'm a drunk." Not all of them say that, of course, but some do. And not everyone says to themselves, "I'm in love," but I did.

It was at the end of my second day at the auction house. Although Hermione and I were working in the same department, I saw little of her in that first day or two, as she had immediately been assigned the task of doing research on a painting that somebody had brought in for valuation. Most of the paintings that came in the door unannounced were of no interest, and there was one member of staff who did the initial screening of these. He was the most tactful person in the building, or so everyone said, and he could turn people away with such skill that most of them went off feeling better than they had when they came in. They still had their painting, of course, and knew that it was not going to be accepted for auction, but somehow they managed to be pleased with this result. Nobody ever worked out exactly how he did it; somebody suggested that it was through a subtle form of hypnotism; others said it was simple charm.

But even if most of those who came in from the street were turned away, nobody was ever discouraged from bringing things in. Stories were told of how a few years earlier a Rembrandt drawing had been brought in by a woman who was carrying it in a plastic shopping bag, along with some sausages bought in the supermarket. And then there was the Turner watercolour that somebody else had been keeping in a biscuit tin. The tin was not quite large enough, and so the owner had folded the edge of the Turner. "I had to," she said. "You have to keep these things in a tin, you know. The light damages them."

The painting that Hermione had to investigate had been consigned by a dealer who had a good idea of what it was, but confirmation was needed. The artist was known, but the auction house did not have any of the literature. That was in the library of the Courtauld Institute, where there were some articles on his work in an obscure German art history review. Hermione read German, and was asked to go and look through these to see if there was anything that might help the senior members of the department to make a firm attribution. They wanted to promote the painting from "attributed to" status. This was where the auction house said that the painting was probably by the artist to whom they attributed it, but they were not saying that it definitely was. "Attributed to" was not a bad status to have, and was better than "Circle of" or "Follower of," but it made a big difference to the price if they could commit firmly to a particular painter.

Hermione told me about her assignment. I felt envious. "Proper work," I said.

She smiled at me. "You'll get some too," she said.

I shrugged. I had been given the task of proofreading a catalogue, checking the spelling of artists' names and their dates. She smiled again when I told her about it, and how boring it was, and then she said, "We could go for a drink after work, if you like. I'm going to meet some friends. You could come along too."

I accepted, and for the next couple of hours I analysed every word of her invitation. **If you like** . . . Was that because she was worried that I might think that she was asking me out, and because she did not want me to form that impression? Was she inviting me along because she felt sorry for me; she was off to the Courtauld to do some real research and I was stuck checking the dates of Dutch Golden Age painters—going to the pub would at least give me something to look forward to. And as for the friends she mentioned, were they male or female, or both? And if they were male, or at least some of them, then might one of them be her boyfriend?

She came back from the Courtauld half an hour before we were due to stop work.

"Did you find anything?" I asked.

She showed me a sheaf of photocopied pages. "Screeds of stuff," she said. "And it's all good news."

I felt envious. I had found one minor mistake in the catalogue: an artist who had been born in Haarlem was described as having been born in Delft. I had circled the error in red ink and then I had sat and gazed at it. The red circle, I realised, was the sum total of my achievement that day. Hermione, by contrast, had found information that might add thirty thousand pounds to the price of a painting.

"You still going for a drink?" I tried to sound casual, but I don't think I succeeded.

She looked at her watch. "Is it that time already? Yes, sure. The others can't make it. They texted me." She hesitated. Or, at least, I thought she hesitated. "But we could go."

I shrugged. "Why not?"

She picked up my insouciance. "Unless you've got something else to do."

"No. Nothing," I blurted out.

The pub was an underground journey away, and it was rush hour. We stood next to one another in the train, and at one point, when the driver applied the brakes at the platform, she had to hold on to me in order to regain her balance. I smiled at her, and I think she left her hand on my arm for slightly longer than was necessary. I looked away and saw a small poster poem displayed on the wall of the carriage. **Love requires an Object,** I read, **But this varies so much / Almost, I imagine / anything will do: / When I was a child I / Loved a pumping engine / Thought it every bit as / Beautiful as you.**

"Why are you smiling?"

I pointed to the poster and she peered over my shoulder to read it.

"W. H. Auden," she said, reading the smaller print at the bottom. She looked at me quizzically. "Will anything do, do you think?"

I was not sure.

"You see," she went on. "I don't think I could love **anything** or **anybody**. Surely that cheapens love. The person you love has to be worthy of it, don't you feel?"

"I suppose so." And yet I was thinking of a girl I knew who had loved somebody who had been dishonest and even violent towards her. She had loved him to the point where she denied the lies and the violence.

"Love can blind you to a person's faults," I muttered.

We had reached our station and she bent down to pick up the bag that had been resting at her feet. I watched her, my gaze dwelling on the curves of her figure, on the line of her neck, her shoulders. And then, for a brief few moments, I closed my eyes as if to test the reality of what I felt. It seemed to me to be a miracle that there was somebody like this in this crowded, ordinary train. She did not belong here; she was altogether too exotic a creature to have to endure the indignities of the London Underground. But it seemed to me to be completely appropriate that we were talking about love, because I could think of nothing that I wanted to talk to her about more than love. As we left the carriage, I took her hand, just for a moment or two, and squeezed it. She was surprised, as I was, by my boldness, but I could tell that she did not mind. She returned the pressure, and then we disengaged and joined the throng of people jostling their way onto the escalator.

In the pub she said to me, "I have to tell you something."

The words fell cold about me. She was going to tell me she had a boyfriend; I was sure of it.

"What's his name?"

She frowned. "How did you know?"

My voice was flat. "People like you have boyfriends. They just do."

"Had," she said. "Had. I was going to tell you that we split up two weeks ago. Then I was going to tell you that I'm not sure that I'm ready . . ."

Now it was my turn to say "How did you know?"

"How did I know that you . . . that you . . ."

"Sorry," I said. "Oh sorry."

"What?"

"I can't help it. I've fallen for you. I feel so stupid."

We were sitting opposite one another at a table in the corner of the pub. She leaned forward to take my hand. "But I want you to. I want you to like me."

I said nothing.

"I want you to because . . . well, I just do."

"You're out of my league."

She burst out laughing. "Why?"

"You're this . . . You're Oxford and God knows what else and I'm just a nobody from nowhere in Scotland and . . ."

"I love the way you talk," she said.

"What I say? Or how I say it?"

"The way you say it. That Scottish accent is just so sexy."

"You've been watching too many films."

"Maybe."

We stayed in the pub for an hour. Then she said that she would cook me a meal at her flat if I wanted that. Of course I did. And I stayed there that night. I know you shouldn't talk about your love life because, well, these things are private and it makes her look cheap, which she was not. I'm sorry, too, if I embarrass you, but I seem to be telling you everything and I can't begin to tell you how I felt that night. I shall never forget it. Not one moment of it.

She did not close the curtains—her flat was on the top floor and was not overlooked, except by the sky. I lay there with her—it was a warm night—and because it was summer the night was quite light. I saw a plane crossing the sky, and it seemed to me that I loved that plane, and that sky, and her flat—everything. Love had transformed the world for me. Transformed it.

7

IT WAS MY FIRST EXPERIENCE OF BEING HEAD over heels in love; my only experience, in fact. I had been infatuated with a girl at university, but that had barely lasted three months and the relationship had not progressed very much. She toyed with me; it flattered her, I think, to have somebody who felt that way about her, but she had no intention of getting involved. "What's the point?" she asked on our final date. "This isn't going anywhere."

"Because you don't want it to," I protested. I thought that if only she would give rein to her feelings then it would be different.

"No, you're right," she said. "I don't."

That was no obstacle, in my view. "You could make an effort. You could try."

She smiled patiently. "You don't try with these things. It's either there or it isn't."

"So it isn't there?"

"No. It isn't."

That rejection had the virtue of clarity, and I retired to lick my wounds. A few days later I saw her with someone else. She did not notice me, but I saw her flirting with him and knew that if it hadn't been there with me, then it was definitely there with him.

I thought of going up to her and saying, “Don’t try too hard,” but fortunately lacked the courage. It would have been petty, and she was right, after all; either it was there or it was not.

But this was so different: Hermione seemed to reciprocate my affection. And that was an extraordinary discovery for me, leading to a state of mind that at the time I had difficulty in describing, although I thought about it a lot. I felt around for the word to describe my feelings, and found a whole dictionary of terms to describe such things. Entrancement; rapture; bliss; there were others—all of them somewhat breathless and none of them capturing what was happening to me. Does everybody feel that he is the only one ever to have felt this way?

The world was suddenly immensely valuable. Everything seemed to have more significance; every moment seemed to have a hinterland of possibility: we might go for dinner somewhere; we might just talk; we might lie in one another’s arms in her room in that flat; might watch the clouds again through the skylight. Even London itself—that great, straggling city with its washed-out, second-hand air, was somehow rendered brilliant and exciting. That’s the curious thing about love, isn’t it? It makes very ordinary things seem special. It makes them seem so much more valuable than they really are.

The auction house was the epicentre of this. I could barely wait to go to work each morning. Although we spent our evenings together, I always went back to the flat I was staying in, even if it was late at night. I sensed that she did not want me to stay, and I did not press her to allow it. She would look at her watch and sigh. "I have to get up early tomorrow."

"Of course. Me too. That's the worst thing about working in London. You have to spend so much time travelling. In Edinburgh you can walk to work from where you stay."

"This isn't Edinburgh."

"No."

She looked at her watch again.

"Tomorrow?" I asked. "What shall we do tomorrow? Not that we have to plan anything. We could just let the day happen . . ." The summer seemed endless. It was only June and we would be together in London until September.

"I don't mind. Anything."

"Go somewhere."

She hesitated before answering. "Would you like to meet my father? I have to see him tomorrow evening. You could come, if you like."

I did not particularly want to meet him, but could hardly refuse. "Of course."

She asked me if I was sure, and I replied that I was. "Why shouldn't I want to meet him? He can't bite my head off, can he?"

She smiled. "You'd be surprised."

"I'm sure he's very nice."

She thought for a moment. "I think he is. But

then he's Daddy." She paused. "From what you've told me, your father was very different. A doctor. Who couldn't like a Scottish doctor?"

I saw him before me, getting into his car, driving away. His death was a matter of tangled metal and pain. It must have been like that, although they had told me—to spare my feelings—that he had died instantly.

"You must miss him," she said. And then, immediately apologising, "Sorry, that's such a trite thing to say. Of course you miss him."

"Every day," I said. "I think of him every day. At least once. Not that I say to myself—time to think about my father. It's not like that. He just comes to mind. Somebody says something. Or I hear something to remind me of him. There's a pipe tune, for instance, 'Mist-Covered Mountains.' I don't think you'll know it, but it's very beautiful. Haunting, really. He loved it. And I hear it sometimes—a few bars of it in my mind, as if somebody were playing it somewhere, and I think of my father."

She reached out to touch me. "Do you think it'll be like that forever? For the rest of your life?"

"I suppose it happens. People can think of somebody every day of their lives. Lots do, I suspect."

She moved closer to me. She had an odd way of looking at me, intensely, as if to place me under particular scrutiny, searching for visual clues as to what was going on in my mind.

"You might not like my father. He's the sort who

rubs some people up the wrong way. He's an alpha male. There was even a newspaper article about him once that called him that. Mr. Alpha, it said."

I laughed. "I've met lots of alpha males."

"Oh?"

"Yes. Bullies and so on . . ." I stopped myself. "Not that your father's a bully. I'm not saying that."

She had not taken offence. "What you said about thinking about somebody every day of your life. I think that's rather sweet . . ."

8

DAVID HAD REACTED WHEN ANDREW HAD made his remark about thinking about somebody every day of his life. He had stiffened briefly and then had smiled. It was a private smile; not one intended to signal anything to the others.

Oh yes, he said to himself. Oh yes, you do. You do. You think about somebody. He fills your world. He is all about you, a presence, and you think about him; you can't help it, because he's always there, in your thoughts. But you know, of course, that all the while you're thinking about him, he's not thinking about you. That's the hardest thing about it. That's what makes it so very, very hard to bear. So hard that sometimes you just sit there and let the misery wash over you; the misery, the emptiness. It's like a great white sea—one of those inland seas you see pictures of in the **National Geographic;** seas that are completely still, seas too salty to have waves or currents. Seas of tears.

9

WE LEFT WORK TOGETHER THE NEXT DAY AS she had said that we would have to catch a train to her father's place. It was forty minutes outside London, she said, in one of those places that is technically outside the city, but is not in the real countryside—a place of trees and lanes that negotiated their way past high hedges intended to shield the houses on the other side from view, but which afforded occasional glimpses of the luxury they almost concealed.

Hermione's mother lived in France, she said. She had gone off a few years earlier with another man—one of her father's closest friends. "They don't speak. They write to one another through their lawyers. Not that there's much to say—it's mostly threats, I think."

"I'm sorry."

"She's much happier, though. She told me their marriage was a nightmare."

I hesitated to say anything. The house was not far from the railway station, and we were walking. There was loose gravel on the pavement—small chips of it from some road repairs, and it made a pleasant, crunching sound. I had walked on gravel before, but never walked on gravel **with her**.

At last I said, "It must be awful to be that unhappy in a marriage."

"Yes."

"Like being in prison," she went on. "And then suddenly it's over and you're free."

"I suppose so."

"They're both happier now," she said. "Although I don't think my father really cares one way or the other. I'm not sure that he was all that unhappy anyway; he didn't really notice my mother. She was just there. He wasn't nasty to her—or not as far as I could see. He just ignored her."

I said that I thought that some people would feel that ignoring somebody amounted to being nasty—certainly it could amount to unkindness, could it not?

"Some people don't know when they're being unkind," she said. "I think my father's one of them. His mind is on other matters. Business mostly."

I had never asked her what he did. I was worried that she would think that I was interested in her for her money—if they had it, which I imagined they did. I had read somewhere about how wealthy people are very discreet and are always concerned that people are going to befriend them for their money rather than for themselves. But now that she had mentioned his business, I brought it up.

"He owns a newspaper," she said. "But that's not

the only thing. It's for his ego. He's the chairman of an investment firm. You see their ads all over the place. I think that's the bit that really matters to him."

I nodded. Newspaper proprietorship was exactly right for a real alpha male—so much so that it almost amounted to a cliché.

"I can see what you're thinking," she said.

I blushed. "I wasn't . . ."

"No, you were. And I don't mind. You were thinking that he owns a newspaper because that's what somebody like him wants to do. People like that own newspapers or football teams. It's about power, isn't it?"

"Maybe. But, look, I can't say very much about it. How can I? I haven't even met your father."

"You soon will," she said.

We had reached a gate. There was a buzzer that she pressed to open the gate. A voice from a small speaker above the button said, "Hermione, darling." It was a man's voice.

She leaned forward to the microphone. "Daddy."

The gate was unlocked from within the house. There was a quiet click. **Well-oiled machinery,** I thought.

She turned to smile at me encouragingly. "Come on."

I SAW IMMEDIATELY THAT HE LOOKED A BIT like her. That was disconcerting at first, because you love a face and then discover that the thing you love is in another face. I know I'm not putting that very well, but it's a very odd feeling. You feel that you should love the other person too—if only a little, out of gratitude.

He looked at me in the same way in which she sometimes did—that same intense stare. That was another thing she got from him.

"So you're Andrew. They call you Andy, no doubt."

"Sometimes. But I like my full name."

It sounded rude, which is exactly the opposite of the effect I had intended. I felt far from confident in the presence of Hermione's father; I was out of my depth, and I knew it. I noticed him react. The intense stare faded and he glanced briefly at Hermione before his gaze turned back to me.

"Of course," he said evenly. "You should never fool around with somebody's name. Names are very important."

"Daddy's called Peter," said Hermione. "I call him Hosh."

"A family nickname," he said quickly. It was a clear invitation not to call him Hosh.

We were standing in the drawing room, a large formal room that looked out onto an expanse of lawn. At the far end of the grass there was a summerhouse, a small wooden structure with a shingled roof. I could see chairs inside and what looked, from where I was standing, as if it was a stuffed bear.

I glanced around the room. It was as different from our living room at home as it could be. My eyes alighted on a picture above the fireplace, a large post-impressionist framed in one of those wide gilt frames that the works of the impressionists and their successors so often appear in. Hermione noticed my glance.

"Bonnard," she said.

I nodded.

"Of course that's what you do, isn't it?" said Peter. He looked at the painting. "I've always liked Bonnard. I bought that in New York. Sotheby's, not your bunch."

"It's lovely," I said.

"A woman in a bath," Peter said. "It must have been difficult being married to Bonnard. Always wanting to paint you in the bath. No privacy at all."

"She might have been flattered," said Hermione.

Peter shrugged. "Maybe." He turned to me. "And what's the art market doing right now? Jittery, like everybody else?"

I tried to remember what somebody had said over coffee the previous day. "It's all right," I said. "Contemporary art is doing rather well. Chinese too."

He smiled, and I wondered whether he had guessed that this was just the recitation of something I had heard from somebody who really knew what he was talking about. But I was not the cause of his smile; it was the fortunes of contemporary art. "Interesting," he said. "I read the other day—it was in the **FT,** I think—there was a report about how one of these chaps, a big name in art today, didn't sell when they put a whole stash of his work up for auction. Nobody wanted it. Because it was rubbish."

He waited for me to react. Presumably he thought that I approved of contemporary installation art.

"I don't like that sort of thing myself," I said.

He stared at me. "Koons and that crew?"

"I don't particularly like Koons' work. I saw something of his that looked like an air conditioner."

He laughed; he was visibly relaxing. "Probably was. Five million dollars?"

"Something like that."

"Created value," he said. "The collectors keep the prices up. The stuff has only scrap value, but they can't let people think that."

"Dutch tulips." I had just read about that.

He looked at me with heightened interest. "The best example there ever was. Although, frankly, I'm surprised the Dutch behaved that way. They were a sensible bunch—solid traders—and then they suddenly went wild over tulip bulbs."

He turned to Hermione. "Mrs. Thing has made dinner for us," he said.

She explained. "Mrs. Thing has got a name, Andrew. Mrs. Dallas. Daddy calls her Mrs. Thing."

He shrugged. "She doesn't mind. I wouldn't call her Mrs. Thing if she minded."

"She's a really good cook," Hermione continued.

Peter moved towards a drinks trolley against the wall behind him. "Something to drink?" he asked. "Mrs. Thing wants us to eat in fifteen minutes or her soufflé will collapse. She always threatens us with collapsed soufflés, but never makes them. It's a peculiarity of hers."

He mixed us drinks and then, while we drank them, he quizzed me. At first the questions were of the sort that might be asked in any friendly conversation, but then they developed an edge. Did I think that my school education had prepared me adequately for university? Did I really think that university degrees needed to be as long as they were, or could they be compressed into two years, or even one? Were my professors there simply because they couldn't do anything else?

I could have been more forceful in their defence, and would have been—in different circumstances. "They're good at their job," I said quietly.

He raised an eyebrow. "Maybe. But it all sounds a bit easy to me. What time do they start in the morning? When do they go home in the evening?"

"I think they're there all day."

He lifted his glass to his lips. "And you? Do you work a full day?"

Hermione shot him a glance, but he ignored it.

Now he answered his own question. "I'm sure you work very hard." He paused. "Art history's certainly interesting. You want to work in an auction house, I take it?"

I told him that I had not made up my mind yet.

"You could work in a museum or gallery, I suppose." He looked at me with amusement.

I swallowed hard. I felt vulnerable. There was a note of condescension in his tone—something that was almost a sneer—and now I knew why Hermione had felt that she had to warn me. Her father was unlikeable—it was as simple as that. I did not like him at all, and I imagined how most people who came across him would think that way.

"Those jobs are quite hard to get," I said mildly.

He smiled. "And that, of course, is why the pay's so low. Jobs that lots of people want to do—and that anybody can do, of course—will never be paid well. Supply and demand."

I felt my heart thumping within me. I had to say something. "Money's not everything," I said. "There's job satisfaction . . ."

"I think you'll find that money **is** everything," he retorted.

Hermione came to my rescue. "I'm with Andrew on that," she said. "You can't put a monetary value on everything." She was polite enough, but I could tell that she was both irritated and embarrassed. I had never been ashamed of my parents, but I knew that there were people who were, and Hermione must have been one.

Her father turned to her with a condescending smile. "Can't you?"

"No," she said. "You can't. And anyway, we need to eat. Mrs. Thing . . ."

"Yes," said her father, putting down his glass and standing up. "We must consider Mrs. Thing."

As we went into the dining room, I glanced at my watch and worked out that we had another two hours of his company.

WALKING BACK TO THE RAILWAY STATION AT half past nine, Hermione slipped her hand in mine. "You did really well."

"He's not too bad." He was, of course. He was worse than I had imagined—a parody, almost, of the condescending magnate, sure of himself, dismissive of those he considered beneath him, arrogant in the core of his being. I had never met anybody like him before, and so I did not understand, as I understand now, that such attitudes speak to weakness far more frequently than they speak to strength.

"That's kind of you. He's not everybody's cup of tea, but he's got his good points."

I waited for her to enumerate them, but nothing came.

"He's got a lot of enemies in the business world," she said. "I think it's his style. He picks fights." She squeezed my hand. "He was trying to pick a fight with you—you realised that, didn't you?"

"I'm not sure. There were things he said . . ."

"That question about whether you worked a full day. I could see what you were thinking."

"Maybe."

She squeezed my hand again. "He'll try to get rid of you," she half whispered.

I let my astonishment show. "You mean he'll try to kill me?"

She giggled. "Oh no, nothing that crude. He'll just try to stop . . . to stop us. He'll do all sorts of things to put a wedge between us. He won't want you to stay with me."

I asked her why. Was it jealousy, or was it because he did not think I was good enough for her?

She thought about her answer for a moment. A breeze had arisen suddenly, a warm breeze, and on it was a trace of some highly scented plant in one of the gardens. It was a scent I knew from our garden at home, but I could not remember the name of the flower.

"Mostly because he won't think you're good enough. Sorry, but you asked. It's difficult to explain."

"Wrong background? Not grand enough?"

She looked down at the ground. "Yes. And money . . ."

"I don't have enough?"

She looked resigned. "Money's everything to him. You heard what he said."

"And what about you? What do you think?"

Perhaps I sounded offended, because she stopped and put her arms about my shoulders. "I wouldn't care if you were ten thousand pounds in debt. Twenty thousand. I don't care in the slightest. I like you, you see; **you.**"

I took her hand. "He made me feel . . . rather inadequate."

"That's what he does to everyone."

"Perhaps he should look out in case somebody kills **him** . . ."

I immediately regretted saying that. She frowned, and then turned away. "I still love him, you know."

I tried to make up for it. "Of course you do. And I'm sorry."

"I've tried to imagine life without him," she said. "I've tried to imagine what it would be like if he . . . if he just weren't there . . . if he just went away. But . . ."

"But he doesn't go away."

"No."

"And you wouldn't want that, anyway, would you?"

She shook her head.

"You need him, I suppose. Your life would be very different if it weren't for him."

She looked at me reproachfully. "It's not just his money . . ."

"I didn't mean that," I said quickly.

"Does it matter to you that . . . that I'm rich?"

"I thought people with money never used that word. And no, it makes no difference." I stared at her. She looked miserable. "You said that it didn't matter to you that I didn't have a penny to my name. Well, same for me, the other way round."

It was a strangely intimate conversation, this talk of fathers and money. I bent down to kiss her. She opened her lips. We kissed twice, three times and then we heard the train approaching. We were still a short distance from the station, and so we disengaged and ran the last little distance. The wheels of the train made a strange sound as it approached—a ringing, humming sound, like the sound of metal strings being played with a great bow; or the sound made by a massive singing bowl, one of those brass bowls that Tibetan monks have and that resonate when the rim is rubbed with a finger. A note is emitted that stretches off into the musical distance, sending shivers up the spine; a train and a singing bowl and a sky above that was still light, but fading and bore witness to the feelings I had for her. I wanted to say, **Forget your father; just forget him. Come with me. We'll go away. Away from him and all of this.**

What would she have said? I did not imagine that she would agree, as the bonds between father and daughter must surely be far stronger than anything I could offer her, who had known her for only a couple of weeks. But people don't necessarily think that way when they are in love. The new lover, of a few weeks standing, may seem more precious than friends of decades. I felt like that about her.

We returned to London. The next day at work, something very odd happened.

10

I WAS CALLED TO A MEETING WITH TWO OF the senior members of my department. These were people I had met but not really had anything much to do with—one of them was on holiday when I had started and had only recently returned; the other had spoken to me once or twice, and had been polite enough, but had given me the impression that interns were, at most, a necessary nuisance—something one had to put up with.

The more senior of the two, the one who had been on holiday, was called Eleanor; her colleague, the one who was unenthusiastic about interns, was called Geoffrey. Eleanor said to me that there was a small collection that had been consigned for sale and that needed cataloguing. It was not an important sale—day sales were reserved for paintings that would not be expected to attract the major buyers; paintings that might be good enough in their way, but that would never be talked about much or take a prominent place on the walls of galleries. They were going over the ten paintings involved and would be happy for me to draft the initial catalogue entries. Of course they would have to approve the final text, but there would be a small amount of research that

I could undertake. It was an advance on the proofreading that I had done earlier on, and I accepted the task with gratitude.

"The owner has a rather inflated idea of the importance—and value—of these paintings," Eleanor said. "But everyone is like that, I suppose. All of us think that whatever we have is better than it actually is, don't you think?"

I asked her whether she was referring to life in general.

"Yes," she replied, smiling. "We like to put the best possible gloss on our lives, I'd say. Look at the way people describe their houses. Or their children for that matter."

"But there must be at least some people who are honest about these things."

She laughed. "Name one." It was as if she was expecting me to reply. "No? Well, let me tell you, collectors always inflate their paintings' attributions. Always."

"So there's nothing important in this collection—the one we're going to be looking at."

For a moment she looked rueful. "Not really. It's solid enough, but nothing to cause much fluttering of hearts in the auction room." She looked at her watch. "Ten o'clock? In my room. The porters are bringing them up now."

When I arrived at ten, Geoffrey was already there. He glanced at me when I came into the room and muttered something in response to my good morning. I think that Eleanor picked up his indifference. She looked at me quickly and I sensed that she disapproved.

"Andrew will be helping us," she said. "He's going to draft the catalogue entries."

Geoffrey turned to me. "Fine," he said. "It's a bit of a rag-bag, I'm afraid." His tone was slightly friendlier now, but I still felt he doubted whether I really needed to be there.

Eleanor had ordered coffee and she made a point of giving me a cup before she gave one to Geoffrey. "So," she said, "let's take a look at what we have here."

The porters had stacked the paintings, three or four deep, against one of the walls of her office. At Eleanor's request I went over and put the first of them on an easel that had been set up at the side of her desk. It was not a large painting, but the frame was ornate and heavy.

"Let me know if you need any help," said Geoffrey, sitting back in his chair and sipping at his coffee.

"I'll be all right."

"Don't drop anything," said Eleanor. "Who was that young man, Geoffrey, who broke that lovely Dutch frame? A couple of years ago?"

Geoffrey shrugged. "The interns fade into one another, I'm afraid." He looked at me and made a falsely apologetic face. "Sorry."

Eleanor noticed this. "And we probably all look the same to them," she said.

It was a gentle reproof, but Geoffrey seemed unmoved by it. Gesturing towards the painting, he passed his judgement. "Not a bad painting. Looks like Gimignani to me."

"I was thinking the same," said Eleanor. "But which one?" There were, I learned, two of them: father and son.

"Giacinto, I think. The father. Not Ludovico."

I stood back and looked at the painting. A group of shepherds was standing under a tree, one of them cradling a baby. The baby was staring out of the picture, so positioned that his eyes would meet those of anybody standing directly in front of the painting.

"That baby looks confused," I said.

Geoffrey glanced at me. "The finding of the infant Paris," he said. "And yes, infants often look confused, not to say miserable, in art. They're usually wondering why they're there."

"A good question for all of us," said Eleanor.

Geoffrey raised an eyebrow. "Very Delphic this morning, aren't we, my dear?"

There was an undercurrent between them, but I was not sure what it was. Professional jealousy? Or was it something else—something more personal?

Eleanor turned to me. "Do you like it, Andrew?"

I hesitated. I was feeling a bit more confident

now, but I was still aware of the fact that they knew everything, it seemed, and I knew next to nothing. I ventured an opinion on the technical skill of the artist and on the composition, which I said I found very pleasing. The shepherds balanced the centurions, I suggested.

Eleanor nodded encouragingly. "Always trust your judgement," she said. "It's the best thing you can do in this business. Trust what your eye tells you. If it says the painting's good, then the painting's good." She turned to Geoffrey.

"Agree with that?"

Geoffrey nodded. "You need an eye." He looked back at me. It occurred to me that he resented her support for a junior member of staff, and that if I was not careful I would be making an enemy. People liked to recruit others, I reminded myself, and perhaps Eleanor was enrolling me on her side against Geoffrey. "Tell me, what else do you see here?"

I looked at the painting again and wondered whether there was something about the sky I should notice. "Perhaps . . ."

He cut me short. "Over-painting," he said curtly. "Here, here and here. See?"

I peered at the places he had pointed out. Now that I looked more closely, it was obvious. I should have picked it up.

"Yes . . . ," I began.

Again he interrupted. "It's fairly obvious, I would

have thought. The surface of the paint is a bit higher and rougher."

"I see . . ."

Had Eleanor seen the over-painting? She must have. He had described it as fairly obvious—was that a barb?

He turned to her. "An estimate of forty to fifty thousand? What do you think?"

She nodded her assent and signalled for me to remove the painting and put the next one on the easel.

"Ah!" said Geoffrey. "I see this is listed as by our friend Dughet. I think I can support that."

"Yes," said Eleanor. "Fairly typical."

She looked at me. "You know about Dughet, Andrew?"

I was pleased to be asked. This would give me a chance to make up for my failure to spot the obvious over-painting in the Gimignani.

"Poussin's brother-in-law and pupil?"

Eleanor seemed pleased. "Yes. Exactly. The National Gallery hangs him next to the Poussins. He called himself Poussin, of course, as you probably know."

I did. "Good career move."

She laughed. "He was never the painter his brother-in-law was, but he was a solid disciple. His skies are very Poussinesque."

Geoffrey sniffed. "Of course he was the more

enthusiastic landscape painter. Poussin was more interested in classical mythology at the point that he was teaching Dughet. So the skies may have come from Dughet rather than Poussin himself."

She hesitated. "Possibly. Possibly. But see that village on the hill—that must have been painted countless times."

"There's always a call for Italian hill towns," said Geoffrey. He leaned forward and examined a figure in the foreground. "Another shepherd. Very pastoral." Turning to Eleanor, he told her what he thought the painting might fetch. They discussed that for a while, and then we moved on to the next picture. But my eye seemed drawn to the Dughet, and even when we were discussing the rest of the paintings, I kept glancing at it again as it rested against the office wall. There was something there that was not quite right, but I could not work out what it was.

At the end of the meeting, I asked whether I could take a photograph of the Dughet. "It interests me," I said.

Eleanor shrugged. "Yes, of course. You can take a look at any of them again while you're preparing the draft. They'll be downstairs."

"When you write the entry for that Dughet," said Geoffrey, "make sure that you mention the Gaspard Poussin aspect. It always attracts attention from people who would like to own a Poussin but who could never afford one. There are lots of them."

I imagined the hosts of those who yearned to

own a Nicholas Poussin but who could only aspire to Gaspard; dissatisfied, restless, feeling bad about themselves because they would never have a real Poussin . . .

"Why are you smiling?" asked Eleanor.

"I was thinking of the Poussinless," I said.

Eleanor grinned. "They are always with us," she muttered. "Isn't that how the saying goes?"

Geoffrey looked at her blankly. Then it dawned on him. "Like the poor?"

She nodded. "Like the poor, Geoffrey."

"Nobody says that any more, my dear. So I would suggest it's a **said**—past tense—rather than a saying."

He was pleased with this joke. Eleanor glanced at me, and I could tell what her glance meant.

11

THE AUCTION HOUSE HAD A LIBRARY AT THE back of their building. It was not a large room, but by covering every inch of wall space with shelves the firm had managed to contain a collection of books and journals that was adequate for much of the research we needed to do. I used the library in preference to the desk I was given in a room shared with the other interns and one of two of the more recently appointed junior staff. I did this because I found it disconcerting to work in the same room as Hermione; I simply could not concentrate if she was there. I think that she felt the same about sharing a room with me, and by tacit consent we fell into a system of my working in the library if she needed to be in our shared office, and if she needed to be in the library I would resume my place in the office.

That afternoon I sat in the library and stared at the photograph of the Dughet I had taken that morning. I had transferred the picture to my laptop, and this enabled me to blow up sections in order to examine them in much greater detail than would have been possible with the naked eye. I started with the figure of the shepherd, and then progressed to the sky. There was nothing exceptional in any of this, but then I looked at the picture in its entirety. It was at this point that I realised what it was that was troubling me: something was happening in the background, in a small section of landscape below the hillside. There was something there: not just trees and the shining surface of a lake, but a puff of white smoke, tiny but unmistakeable. And beneath it, the source of the smoke, a minuscule black pipe that on closer examination revealed itself as being the funnel of a steam train.

For a few moments I stared at this in disbelief. This was impossible. This was a painting executed in the first half of the seventeenth century by an artist who had never seen a steam train. Yes, Leonardo da Vinci drew helicopters, but he was an exception, and his helicopters were never more than an idea.

I looked again. Was I imagining it? No, whichever way I peered, I reached the same conclusion. There was a steam train in this picture of Italian arcadia.

I walked briskly from the library—almost ran. Hermione was alone in our shared office, and I thrust my laptop in front of her. "Do you mind!" She pushed the computer away from the papers she had in front of her.

"Sorry," I said, "but you have to take a look."

She peered at the enlarged section on the screen. "So?" she said. "A train. So?"

I reduced the magnification so that the rest of the painting came into focus.

She frowned. "Poussin?"

"Gaspard Dughet—brother-in-law of Nicholas Poussin. But that's not the point."

She looked puzzled. "What is the point then?"

"The seventeenth century. **Seventeenth**. And this is a train. A steam train."

She smiled. "Sorry, my mind was elsewhere. It's a mistake, then. This can't be Dughet, or whatever you call him."

I sat down next to her. Her leg touched mine briefly, and for a moment I stopped thinking about Dughet and steam trains. We would go out for dinner that night, I decided. I would dip into my dwindling funds and take her out to dinner.

I came back to the picture. "I think they're wrong. They said it was definitely Dughet—I was at the meeting. It was Eleanor—you know, that nice woman—and that Geoffrey character."

"Can't stand him," said Hermione.

"They both said it was Dughet. There seemed to be no doubt in their minds."

Hermione looked again at the picture on the screen. "It's easy enough to miss it, I suppose. It's a very small part of the overall picture and . . ."

"Yes," I said. "I agree. We can all miss things. But

Geoffrey jumped down my throat for missing over-painting in another painting. Now here he is doing the same thing himself."

"He's not going to like it."

She was right. I could imagine Eleanor being amused to discover that she had missed something so obvious, but Geoffrey's likely response was another matter altogether.

Hermione looked at me quizzically. "You are going to tell them, aren't you?"

I wanted to say no. I wanted to say that the last thing I wished to do was to challenge my employers. But I realised what she would think of me if I said that, and so I plucked up my courage. "Of course."

She seemed relieved. "Good. You couldn't let them be shown up. What if somebody spotted it at the viewing—and they're bound to. It would be very embarrassing for the firm."

I swallowed hard. "I suppose I should go and speak to them straight away." I paused. "And dinner tonight?"

She shook her head. "I'd love to but . . ." She tailed off.

I waited for her to complete the sentence.

"But my father has asked me to meet him at the Savoy."

"Oh." I could not think of anything else to say, and so I said, "For dinner?"

"Yes. And I really feel that I should."

"Of course you should." I tried to conceal my disappointment, but it must have showed.

"I hope you don't mind," she said. "I'd far rather have dinner with you."

I did mind. I was not included in the invitation, and I remembered what she had said. **He'll try to get rid of you**.

"Please don't talk about me," I blurted out.

"I won't. I promise you." She looked concerned. "So what will you do?"

I said the first thing that came into my mind. "Read."

"What are you reading?"

My hesitation made it clear that I had not been intending to read.

"You're angry with me," she said.

"Of course I'm not angry. Why should I be angry?"

"Because I'm having dinner with him. And you'll be all alone."

I became brisk. "With only ten million people in London, or whatever it is? No, I'll meet up with a friend. We can go to the pub."

She looked at me. I think that she was about to ask me which friend I had in mind, but then she realised that would be as tactless as asking which author I had been reading.

I looked at my watch. Eleanor had said something about being in a meeting until about three that afternoon but that I could get back to her thereafter with any questions about the catalogue entries. It was not long after three; I would go to see her and tell her, rather than Geoffrey, about my discovery.

12

SHE LISTENED ATTENTIVELY. THEN SHE SAID, "Let's take a look. I'll get somebody to bring the painting up straight away."

I was anxious to apologise for bringing the matter up. "Maybe I'm wrong," I said, "but it just looks so like a train to me. I don't see what else it could be."

She laughed, pointing to the photograph I had shown her. "Neither do I. It's a train. I think so too—in which case you've saved us considerable embarrassment."

She called through to the porters' office and asked for the Dughet to be brought up. Then she made another call. "I'll get Geoffrey in."

I tried not to wince, but she noticed my reaction.

"He's all right," she reassured me. "He's very good at his job, you know, but I can see how junior staff find him a little bit . . . how should we put it? Daunting? But you shouldn't really. He can teach you a lot."

She made the call, and Geoffrey was summoned. The painting, though, arrived before he did, and we had a chance to examine it together.

"You're absolutely right," Eleanor said. "It's a train. And that makes this a nineteenth-century painting by a follower of Dughet, I'd say. A follower, perhaps, with a sense of humour . . ."

Geoffrey came into the room. He seemed surprised to see me there and he threw an enquiring glance at Eleanor.

"Andrew has discovered something rather interesting," she said. "He's found out that we might be wrong about that Dughet."

Geoffrey frowned. "Oh?"

Eleanor looked at me. "You show him, Andrew."

Geoffrey came and stood next to me, beside the painting. I was strongly aware of his physical presence; I heard his breathing, which was slightly raspy. He was overweight, and obviously unfit. It suddenly occurred to me that he might have a heart attack. I would point out the train and he would have a heart attack in response.

"There's a train here," I said. "Look."

He bent down to examine the painting. The breathing became more audible.

He stared at the painting for a few minutes. Then he shifted his position and looked at it from a slightly different angle. He touched the canvas gently, as a doctor might touch a patient. Then he stood up.

"Obviously over-painted," he said. "Some enthusiastic owner in the nineteenth century decided that a train would improve matters."

My mouth dropped open.

"Yes," he said. "You should mention that in your note, Andrew. It might add to the interest." He paused. "It's still Dughet, Eleanor."

His tone was firm, but Eleanor looked doubtful. "Are you sure?" She leaned forward and then moved to look at the painting from a different angle. "It seems quite smooth. I can't see anything from this side . . ."

"Well, I can," he said. "Look from here. Come and stand here and then look across the surface. See the change in shade of black. No doubt about it. None at all."

She frowned, and then straightened up again. She looked unhappy. "Yes, I see what you mean."

I could tell that he was irritated, and had been only slightly mollified by Eleanor's acceptance of his view. He turned to me. "You didn't doubt the attribution, did you?"

I held his gaze. "Actually, I wondered . . ."

"Well, you were wrong."

Eleanor came to my rescue. "Andrew did the right thing to raise it."

He shrugged. "Perhaps."

I left the two of them in her office. They would be discussing me. That evening, Hermione's father would also be discussing me—or would want to do so, even if Hermione objected. I suddenly felt homesick. I wanted to be back in Scotland. I wanted to go home. But then I thought of Hermione, and

I decided that I would ask her to marry me. I had not known her for very long—I accepted that—but that was not the point. The point was that I could think of nothing I wanted more than to be with her for the rest of my life. Nothing else counted.

I went back to the library and took a piece of headed paper from a drawer. **I love you more than I can say,** I wrote. **I love you so much. Let's go off somewhere together. Anywhere. Why not? Please say yes. Say yes. Just yes. Not maybe. Just say yes. That's all you have to do.** And then I added: **Go on, marry me!**

I put the letter in an envelope and wrote **Hermione** across the front. Then I went back to our shared office. She was not there, but was obviously going to return shortly, as there was a half-finished cup of coffee on the desk. A tiny whisper of steam arose from the still-warm surface of the liquid like the smoke of a miniature steam train—as insubstantial, as transient as that.

I left the envelope on her desk, propped up against a box-file. Then, ten minutes later I ran back into the office, brushing past a secretary who was walking along the corridor. She looked at me venomously. "Don't be so rude," she muttered. She was right—it was rude, but I had to get the letter back.

It was still there, unopened. I was tearing it up when Hermione came into the room. Her eyes went straight to the fragments of paper that slipped from my hand and fluttered to the ground.

"Nothing," I blurted out, in an attempt to forestall her question.

She smiled. "I didn't say anything." But then she added, "Second thoughts?"

13

DAVID HAD BEEN LISTENING INTENTLY TO Andrew's story; he would have liked Hermione to say yes to Andrew—had she seen the letter, which was not at all clear—but thought, on balance, she would not have done. She would have been more sensible than that, he imagined—how long had they known one another? A few weeks? You did not accept a proposal after a few weeks; not if you had any sense. But of course there were plenty of people with very little sense when it came to these matters—judgement deserted them as they persuaded themselves the discouraging statistics somehow did not apply to them. This was a summer romance, and summer romances by definition never lasted beyond September. It was touching, but that was all it was: two young people meeting one another and falling in love for a few months; it happened all the time. At the end of the summer they would have to go back to Edinburgh and to Oxford, two different worlds. And then there was the father. He wondered about him. Hermione would be loyal to him, he suspected, but only to a point: there would come a time at which she would choose a lover rather than a parent. Biology dictated that.

He looked at his travelling companions and said to himself: **I would like to tell them about me**. But he felt that he could not, because it would be hard to do so; it was never easy to speak about this to complete strangers, which was what they were. And so he thought for a while about what he would say if he were able to speak. They would understand, he expected; people understood now, but not everybody did, and that sometimes made it difficult. The problem was that people **pretended**. It was not unlike the issue they were talking about earlier on—about the adequacy of effort and whether one could try to be brave. People tried to understand, and many did, but not everybody could make the imaginative leap that landed one in the position of another person, in their shoes, in their very garments, looking out on the world with their eyes, feeling what went on inside their hearts; being made to cry by the things that made them want to cry. That was easy in theory, but hard in practice. They pretended to understand, but when it came down to it, many simply did not. They simply did not understand because they could not know—not really know—what it was like to be the other. That was because it was not them. That was why they could not think that. It had to be you.

He remembered that other journey, also by train,

but a rather different one. You could not just hop on a train between Washington and New York, you had to have a ticket and stand in a waiting area before they allowed you access to the platform. It was more like waiting to board a plane—an ordered process so different from rail travel in other countries. He had been a regular visitor to India and had been on one of those trains where people sat on the roof or hung out of the windows of carriages. He had never got used to that, even if he had become inured to the many other indignities of poverty you witnessed there. Did these travellers pay for their perilous journey, he wondered? Was there some sort of ticket, some fourth or fifth class, that allowed you to take your chances on the outside of the train, hoping that you would not lose your grip or be swept off by some obstruction—a signal arm, a wire, a low-slung railway bridge? Perhaps now that air travel was more common, people would try it there, too, clinging on to the wings of planes just as they did to the roofs of trains. He pictured for a moment—absurd thought—a plane so laden, just managing to get airborne because of the human burden on its wings and roof, limping through the sky, barely clearing the tree-tops below, until it eventually landed somewhere and the relieved survivors lowered themselves onto the tarmac and ran off before they could be asked for a fare . . .

At Union Station in Washington he had been early for his train back to New York and had stood for over half an hour in the line waiting for the platform to be readied. He had been standing behind a woman speaking loudly on her cell phone about business arrangements and had been obliged to listen to the details. He had turned his back on her, hoping to blot out the conversation, but had found that this only had the opposite effect. She was a distributor of olives, and was discussing a client's requirements. It was very complicated because the olives came in cartons of twenty jars and there were customers who wanted to order in units other than twenty.

"Tell them they can have forty, sixty, eighty and so on. Multiples of twenty. Tell them that they should round the order up—if they want fifteen, order twenty. Sure, they'll have to hold on to another five jars, but they can sell those. Five jars? You'll always shift five jars. No, tell them we don't split the cartons because then it'd be us with the spare five jars, and we don't have anywhere to put them. Tell them it's not our warehouse—we don't have guys down there to open the cartons and sort out the numbers. We just don't. Those guys work for Edwards not for us. Tell them that."

He tried to detach himself—he tried not to listen. But he found himself picturing the warehouse with its stacked crates of olives, and he could see her point. Of course they couldn't open the crates because you couldn't stack individual jars in a warehouse like that. They'd break, and there would be glass all over the floor, and Edwards' men might slip and cut themselves and there would be litigation and . . . Tell them that, he thought. Tell them about the problems down at Edwards' end. Tell them that some things come in units of twenty—they just do—and we should be grateful that they don't come in units of one hundred. Tell them not to be so demanding . . .

The issue of the olives was resolved and his neighbour began to busy herself with a copy of **The Washington Post,** reading an article with a frown of disapproval; perhaps she was still cross about the unreasonableness of her customers—or at least of some of them. He looked about him, glancing at his fellow travellers, allowing himself to imagine why they were making this particular journey. Going home? Visiting children in New York? A few days in the city: a show on Broadway, an opera at the Met, an over-priced dinner? A meeting? A wedding?

His attention was caught by two new arrivals. Two young men had arrived at the end of the line. One was to board the train, he thought; the other had come to see him off. A suitcase stood at the feet of one of them—a nondescript suitcase with an old baggage label attached to the handle.

He wondered about them. There was a similarity in appearance—both were in their early twenties, if that, perhaps slightly younger—two college boys then. One had shorter hair than the other; one had seen more of the sun than his friend. Their dress was similar, but the one who was travelling had made some effort to look smart.

A loudspeaker crackled into life and people picked up their impedimenta. The woman in front of him folded her newspaper and reached, with a sigh, for the bulging briefcase at her feet. A mother grabbed her son and started to pack away the toy with which the child had been playing; the boy protested loudly, began to cry.

He watched the two young men. They were both tall, but one was slightly taller than the other. They were shaking hands—the taller one was staying—it was the other who was travelling, the one who had been tanned by the sun. The handshake continued, and then one moved forward and embraced the other, hands about shoulders.

He did not move. A guard was preparing to remove the barrier to the platform. He felt somebody's back-pack against his leg. "Sorry. I think that's our train." He paid no attention. The young men still held one another, and then one took a step back and raised a hand in farewell. He watched. There was something strangely moving in this. A line came to him from a poem he had once read: **It is a long disease this separation of broth-**

ers . . . He had forgotten that, but there were words that haunted us and came back out of context, for no particular reason: lines of poetry, of song, of childhood prayer could do that. **Dear Matthew, Mark, Luke and John: Please bless this bed I lie upon;** the childish request so deeply embedded in the recesses of memory, and now emerging unbidden. Or the line from a poem he had once read—words that had stuck in his mind and kept returning: **It is the onion, memory, that makes me cry . . .**

The queue started to move. He picked up his own bag, and then glanced back at the two young men. The one saying goodbye had started to leave, but turned round at that precise moment and waved. But his friend, caught up in the crowd, did not see him.

He looked up at the vaulted ceiling of the great railway station. It was indifferent to parting, he thought. And then he thought: the architecture of farewell. The architecture of love. The architecture of loss.

THE TRAIN MOVED SLOWLY AT FIRST. PEOPLE settled in their places, began the activities that would divert them during the few hours to New York. Books were opened, computers switched on, eyes were shut, with relief, for sleep. He sat unmoving—and stared out of the window. He was thinking of the scene he had just witnessed. People talked of the wrench of parting, and that, he felt, was exactly what it was. Take a metal object off a magnet and one would experience that—there was the draw, the tug, the flow of the bond even through the air, and then the sudden detaching as separation occurred. That was what it was like. That was human parting. You felt it; you felt the separation, just as you would feel the rending of tissue being pulled apart.

He closed his eyes, but did not want to sleep. He wanted to think. He wanted to allow memory to make its own journey, just as he was doing now, travelling from one place to another. First meeting; the long friendship; parting: a journey with saliences and stations of its own.

It's easy to be foolish, he thought. It's dead simple, really. All you have to be is human and to allow yourself to do the human things, like fall in love with somebody when you know that there's no point and when you know, too, that it's just going to make you unhappy. It's better to be stoic—to be one of those people who manage to keep themselves to themselves, who manage to avoid letting go and becoming entangled in something that they know from experience is going to cause unhappiness. Or is it? There were people who chose that, and seemed to do it successfully, but weren't they filled with regret? Inside, where nobody could see, didn't it hurt them to think about what they never had? He thought there were, and that was one thing that he had never suffered from. He had no regrets about this, because what he had had was so important to him that he would never have wished that it had not happened.

14

WHEN HE WAS YOUNG THEY USED TO GO FOR six weeks in the summer to a small town in Maine. It was not one of those fashionable places, popular with politicians and the wealthy, places that could be reached from New York within a couple of hours. This took much longer to reach, and was, as a result, less sought-after as a place for retreat. There was a bigger town nearby that had an airfield, served by a daily plane from Boston, but most people who went there in the summer drove long distances up the coast until they reached the harbour village with its single street of shops and its deserted canning works. There was nothing much else, really, apart from a rickety sawmill that still employed three men and that whined and coughed its way through the lumber that was brought down from the forests in the hinterland.

Their house was one of the last houses in town. Beyond them was an orchard, left to decline and now overgrown with rioting Boyne brambles, a home for scurrying wild creatures. A little way further away was a river, on the banks of which were flat expanses of rock, covered when the water was in spate, but exposed when it was low. Further down, where the river broadened out into an estuary, there were two houses lived in by fishermen and their families. Their boats, white and wooden, bobbed about on moorings in front of their owners' houses. He would watch them set off on the ebb tide and then see them again when they returned from the inspection of their pots. They often caught crabs, a writhing mass of waving claws, but their real quarry was something different. His mother sent him to collect lobster from the fishermen once a week, and he would be given a couple of large specimens, their claws firmly secured by the heavy-duty rubber bands they used for this purpose.

"You don't let one of these fellows get your fingers," said one of the fishermen, showing him a bent index finger on his left hand. "See this? A lobster did that years ago. Snap. Didn't even have to exert himself."

He stared at the lobsters and they stared back, their unreadable black eyes fixed on him. He did not like the way they were killed. He heard their screams and thought that no creature would make that sound if it did not experience pain.

"They don't feel it," said his father. "Lobsters don't feel things."

Adults lie, he thought. They lie about lobsters and a whole lot of other things.

THEY SPENT SIX WEEKS OF EACH SUMMER there. His father owned a small property business in

New York that looked after itself—or so he claimed. In reality, the business was carefully nurtured by its long-term manager, who did all the work and who was given a small share of the profits as a reward. This manager never went away, apparently having no interest in taking a holiday.

"Why leave New York?" he said. "New York's got everything. If you go some place else, you'll end up missing things you have in New York. Better stay where you are. Far better."

The business did well, and funded a large apartment on the Upper East Side as well as this house in Maine. The family did not live extravagantly, money being invested rather than spent. In due course all this went to David. But that was a long way ahead.

His father, he realised, was grateful for this good fortune. "Look at this," he once said to him. "This house. This place. We wake up to the sound of birds. We look out our window at an orchard. If we want fish, we go out and catch them."

This gave him pause for thought. Yes, he understood that this was a good place to be, but he wanted to be elsewhere. He wanted to see the world beyond the boundaries of New England; beyond the boundaries of the United States itself. Africa. India. Australia. There were all these places where the houses were not made of neat white board and shingle; where there was colour and movement and danger. There was no danger in that small town, where people's lives led neatly and correctly to the grave; where the water came dosed with chemicals and the food was cleanly wrapped. He wanted to go somewhere else.

"Yes," said his father. "There are other places—sure there are. Plenty of places to go and get sick because the water's rotten and there's malaria and cholera and so on. There are plenty of places like that."

15

ON HIS FIFTEENTH BIRTHDAY, WHICH FELL in mid-July, when they were always in Maine, he was given a boat. It was delivered to the house at night, when he was asleep, and so it was there as a surprise for him when he woke up. It was a small dinghy, twelve feet in length, made of welded aluminium, and came with a set of varnished pine oars. His heart gave a leap; he had dreamed of possessing a boat, but had always had to make do with the occasional use of boats belonging to neighbours. Now that he had his own, the river and the estuary were his to explore.

"Watch the tides," said his father. "Don't forget how powerful they are. Be careful."

He launched the boat immediately. It sat well in the water and was easy to row, although it had a high freeboard, and was sensitive to the wind. He quickly became used to that, though, and felt safe even when the river was swollen by heavy rains. He used it for fishing, or simply for rowing down towards the estuary, riding the current, and then back up. He liked the sensations involved: the feeling of being borne by the tide, the sound made by the oars as they cut into the water, the thumping sound of wavelets against the curve of the bow, a sound that was like tiny, muffled explosions.

A few weeks after he had first used it, he rowed down the river one afternoon, intending to fish at the point where the fresh water met the salt. Fish seemed to like that confluence, and he might return home with a catch that his mother would use for the evening meal, freshly grilled and served with new potatoes bought from neighbours who had a large vegetable patch.

He rowed out. Rains inland had swollen the river and this, combined with a high tide, made for a broad expanse of water. The sky above was cloudy, and the surface of the water was like milky glass. There would be fish, he thought; they liked such conditions.

He stopped rowing and started to prepare his line. This was absorbing work, and he did not notice that one of the oars had slipped out of its rowlock and fallen into the water. Caught in the current, it drifted away, sufficiently quickly that when he turned and saw what had happened it was well away from the boat.

He put aside the fishing rod and started to use the remaining oar as a paddle. But it was slow work, as the boat swung round with each stroke and made little progress. It was on the edge of the estuary now, and he realised that it would soon be carried out into the sea itself. A gull swooped low to investigate, mewing, curious and hungry.

There was another boat not far away. This had an outboard, and he could see that it was heading for an object in the water—an object that must be his oar. He waved, and the figure crouched in the boat waved back. The engine note changed, and the other boat stopped as the oar was retrieved; then there was a high-pitched buzzing as it turned and headed for him. There was a boy in the boat.

"Here it is," shouted the other boy, throttling back. "Do you need a tow?"

He could have rowed back, but thought that he would accept. A line was thrown and secured to a cleat on the boat's bow.

"Climb in here," said his rescuer. "The engine pulls better if we're low in the water."

He stepped into the other boat and said thank you. This boy, he saw, was about the same age as he was. He was wearing jeans and a red tee-shirt; he was barefoot. He introduced himself as Bruce.

"I've seen you in your boat," he said. "I wondered if you were catching anything."

"It depends," he said. "Sometimes I do. Sometimes not. Like all fishing."

Bruce smiled. "Yes. Like all fishing."

The outboard motor drowned conversation, and they made the rest of the journey without saying anything to one another. When they reached the jetty where David tied his boat, Bruce tied up too.

"I'll come with you to your place," he said. "I've got nothing else to do."

They went home. He introduced his new friend to his parents. Then they drank a soda sitting on the porch, and Bruce told him about how his parents had bought a house nearby but seemed not to get many opportunities to use it.

"They're always busy," he said. "They work all the time."

His father was a professor at Princeton, he explained. He was a mathematician. "He makes mathematical models all the time. He's obsessed. There's only one word for it—obsessed."

David laughed. He said: "Parents need help."

Bruce stayed for an hour, and then announced that he would have to go as he was meeting a girl. He was not sure whether he really liked her, but he thought he did.

"She's obsessed too," he said.

"Obsessed with what?"

Bruce shrugged. "I haven't found out yet."

David looked at him, puzzled.

"I'm kidding," said Bruce. "Half of what I say means nothing. You need to know that."

"Perhaps you're obsessed," said David.

16

THE NEXT DAY HE TOOK THE BOAT OUT again. The river had abated, and the water seemed sluggish. There were no fish, and he turned back after an hour or so on the water. He had hoped that he would see Bruce's boat, but there was no sign of it. After he had tied up at the jetty, he wheeled his bicycle out of the shed and rode it along the main street. There was nowhere to go in the town, apart from a diner that was usually deserted except for at lunchtime and for a brief period in the early evening. He looked in the window of this, wondering whether he might see Bruce with the obsessive girl. He did not.

He had worked out which house it was Bruce's parents had bought, and he rode past this, slowly, snatching a glance at it, again hoping that his new friend might just happen to be coming out of the front door or the driveway, but there was no sign of anybody. There was a large grey car parked under a tree, but nothing else to show the house was occupied.

He imagined the professor of mathematics sitting at his desk at one of the windows creating mathematical models. He imagined Bruce waiting for his father to pay some attention to him. **Parents need help**. He had no idea why he had said that, but it seemed to be the right sort of witty remark to make. There was something about Bruce's company that had made him feel livelier, more perceptive. He had only been with him for an hour or two, but during that brief time it seemed to him that the world had been in some inexplicable way more intense. It was as if the brightness had been turned up.

He went home.

His father said, "That friend of yours came round."

His heart leapt. "Who?"

"Bruce? Is that his name?"

"Yes." He waited. Time had slowed down. It felt buttery. It was strange—he knew that—but that was how it felt to him. Buttery. "What did he say?"

His father shrugged. "Nothing much. He asked where you were and I said that you were off on your bike somewhere."

"And?"

"He didn't say anything. Or he just said, **I have to go**. Yes, I think he said something about having to go."

He nodded and went to his room. He did not want his father to see him, in case he could tell that there was something wrong. He wanted to appear casual—as if a visit by Bruce was nothing to be excited about. But inside, he experienced a joyful, soaring feeling that made him feel dizzy.

He waited an hour before he left. He did not want Bruce to think that he had come round straight away on hearing that he had missed him; rather, he wanted him to think that he had been doing other things and had then decided to repay the call.

He rode round to the house. The large grey car was no longer under the tree, but Bruce answered the door when he rang the bell. He seemed surprised to see him.

"You came round to my place?"

Bruce nodded. "I wondered what you were doing."

"Nothing. I was doing nothing really."

Bruce smiled. He had a wide smile—one that seemed to split the whole lower part of his face. He would try to smile like that himself, because it was the sort of smile that made you feel warm inside. You had to have the right sort of mouth, of course—which Bruce did.

"That's all there is to do here," said Bruce. "Nothing."

"Yes, that's right." He felt disloyal to the village. He had never before thought that there was nothing to do there, but now that Bruce had made the observation, he wanted to agree.

"That's why we're going back to Princeton tomorrow," said Bruce. "My parents get frustrated. They're so obsessive, you see. They need to be doing things."

The words seemed to end his world. "Tomorrow?"

"Yes. We're driving back."

He looked out onto the yard, beyond Bruce's shoulder. There were trees, framed by the casing of the window. The branches were moving slightly, and beyond them was cloud.

17

KAY WAS WONDERING WHETHER DAVID WAS going to say something. He was clearly thinking—the expression of a person deep in thought betrays the fact—but his thoughts, it seemed, were to be private because he had chosen to keep them so. Which is how it should be, she decided, if that was what he wanted; the disclosure of something as intimate as love should not be a matter about which one should feel obliged to speak simply because others were doing so. And yet she herself wished to speak, because what she had to say had a lot to do—everything, in fact—with the reason why she was on that particular train journey. Her father had been Scottish . . . **had been:** his Scottishness had been replaced by another identity altogether. One could do that in Australia, just as one could do that in America or Canada—each of them a place that offered an identity that could be put on, like a new jacket. Her father had stopped referring to himself as a Scotsman and had begun to call himself Australian; such an important step, like putting aside a maiden name, or taking on, as one does in some religious conversion, a name given by the new faith, the name of some saint or prophet.

"My father was Scottish," she said.

David looked at her. Whatever he had been thinking about had been interrupted. "Oh yes?"

"He left Scotland in 1946. That sounds so long ago now, doesn't it, and it was, I suppose. Imagine what the world was like then: a year after the end of the nightmare, after the dropping of those two atomic bombs and the liberation of the camps and, well, all that suffering. The world must have been like a hospital ward, with the wounded and the confused standing around and waiting to find out what was going to happen to them. But perhaps it was a good time to start a new life, particularly if you were nineteen, as he was, and impatient."

David said to her: "Yes, of course. At that time people could just decide where they wanted to go, couldn't they? There was very little red tape. If you wanted to go and live somewhere, you just did. You didn't have to worry about visas and permits and all the rest. You moved. If you had the right citizenship, that is."

She smiled at that. "There was more than red tape for some. There were fences and gates."

"Yes, I suppose there were. But not for your father, I imagine. Half the map was coloured red then. Or was it pink?"

"Red. So he could have chosen. He could have gone to Malaya or Nyasaland or Hong Kong—there were lots of places that would have taken a nineteen-year-old Scotsman who was good with his hands and prepared to work. There were plenty of places where he would have been slotted in. But he went to Australia because of a book he had as a child. It was called **The British Empire in Pictures,** and it showed people doing all sorts of things in exotic settings. He said that there was a picture of an Australian stockman on a horse and this man had turned to the camera and was smiling. He said that there was something in the man's expression that meant something to him, and when you turned the page you saw a picture of people running into the surf on a beach in New South Wales and that tipped the balance.

Imagine being in Scotland, just after the War when there was still rationing and you were hungry and probably cold as well, and you saw these pictures of people riding horses and standing on beaches. Imagine.

MEN NEEDED FOR WESTERN AUSTRALIA. That was all it said. He saw it in the newspaper that his father brought back from work each day, and he might easily have missed it, had he not begun reading a report on page ten that was continued on page twenty-two, where the notice was tucked away alongside other advertisements for cheap suits, pills, sturdy bicycles. The wording might have been terse, but perhaps it said quite enough. There was a place called Western Australia and they needed men there. What more was there to be said? They would need men because everywhere seemed to need men. Too many men had died—unimaginable millions of them—and now they needed men to do the things that those men had done. That, surely, needed no further explanation.

He cut it out and placed it in the pocket of his shirt, and might have forgotten about it had he not found it again that night when he took off his shirt and laid it on the chair in the bedroom he shared with his two younger brothers. They all slept in one bed, which was common in those days, because they were poor and they were lucky not to have to share with their parents as well. There were two beds in the house: the parental bed, which was behind a curtain off the living room, and the children's bed, which was in the other room. They lay like sardines: two heads on a long pillow separated by one set of feet. Turns were taken to be the one in the middle, the feet, and the blanket was used to protect one from elbows and kicking. The youngest of the three boys, who was eight, suffered from nightmares, and cried out in the darkness; something about bombing, which they had never experienced in the Ayrshire town where they lived. There had been bombs in Glasgow, but nothing as bad as the London Blitz, which they had seen in the newspaper pictures, and it had lodged in the mind of the younger boy.

"Alec, do they bomb boys as well? Bairns too?"

This question had been prompted by a picture of a young boy picking over the ruins of a house in London—all tumbled brick and split rafters like sticks of firewood; the boy had been looking for his toys, or the remains of them, the caption said.

"Aye, boys get bombed, too, but not here, Jack. Not here. Nobody's going to bomb you."

"Auld Hitler wadnae waste a decent bomb on you!" This from the middle brother, who was silenced by a threatening look.

That was reassurance, perhaps, but not enough to prevent the nightmares, which woke them all and inevitably brought a parent into the room to comfort the frightened boy. On that evening there had been such a disturbance, and he had lain awake for long hours afterwards, thinking about the advertisement and about Western Australia. He would go. They needed men, and he was now a man, who could do a man's job in Australia, or anywhere else for that matter.

The notice had given the address of an agent in London, and he wrote off the next day. In his letter he explained that he was currently serving an apprenticeship as an electrician, but that he could be released from this and could turn his hand to any job offered him. It was six days before he received a reply; a form was enclosed and he should fill that in. There was a pamphlet describing the benefits available and the terms on which he might be given an assisted passage.

His younger brothers watched him as he filled in the form. They did not want him to leave—he was their brother, their protector—but he assured them that they could come, too, once they were old enough.

"There'll be room for all of us," he said. "It's a big country."

He told his parents. They said that he was an adult now and the decision was his.

"We'll miss you, Alec; of course we will. But you'll be all right. You'll find a nice girl out there and have your own family and we'll come and see you one day maybe . . ."

He could see that they were being brave. Australia was as far away as could be imagined, and everybody knew that when you said goodbye to somebody going to Australia, it was often goodbye forever.

He arrived in Fremantle, on a ship that had called in at Cape Town. The last leg of the journey, across lonely wastes of ocean, had brought home to him how far away he was going. In Cape Town, where more passengers had boarded, passengers on deck had thrown paper streamers down to friends and relatives on the quay below. As the tugs nudged the ship from its berth, these streamers had briefly become taut, brightly coloured links between those on board and those on shore, and then had snapped and fallen graceful and fluttering into the water below. Beside him on the deck, watching the crowds, was an Australian serviceman, weeping with relief at leaving Africa, his hand in a plaster cast from a wound he had received somewhere up north, doing something, he explained, that he should not have been doing, and therefore his own fault. What was Perth like? he asked. The tops, mate. The tops. No doubt about that. None at all.

They met rough seas, and the air below became fetid with the results of sea-sickness. It was everywhere—the acidic smell of sickness; in the corridors, in the dining room, in the cabins themselves. The stewards, overworked, did their best, but many of them were sick themselves and simply added to the problem.

Then it stopped, and the smell of sickness was replaced by the smell of liberally applied disinfectant. People went back on deck, where they played quoits with heavy rubber rings, or sat in deck chairs and stared up at the sun that was so unfamiliar to many of them. It was as if they were escaping a darkness that had lasted for years; for some of them, for all their life.

Fruit had been brought on board at Cape Town: oranges, plums, peaches. There was an abundance that was almost shocking to him, because they had so carefully husbanded their rations back home and had simply not seen fruit. He found himself sucking hungrily at oranges, making a hole in the skin and then squeezing out the contents—the pith, the juice, even the pips. He felt his body react to the jolt of sugars; he felt stronger, he felt more confident.

And then, shortly after dawn one morning, they were in sight of land, a low smudge on the horizon. A deckhand pointed it out to him and said, "That's Fremantle. We'll be there by lunch. You'll be off by three at the latest."

He strained his eyes trying to make out the details, but it was hours before he saw the shape of buildings—a harbour crane, ships at anchor outside the harbour, distant hills. They had been required to stay on board in Cape Town because of a tight sailing deadline, and so he had not gone ashore there. This, then, would be the first land on which he would set foot that was not Scotland or England. He had never been anywhere else in his life.

HE WAS GIVEN A ROOM IN A HOSTEL NEAR the docks. It was hot, and he also found it uncomfortable and noisy. As soon as he could manage it, he answered an advertisement for lodgings with a widow who let her two spare bedrooms to "respectable working men." She looked him up and down, assessing his respectability, and then offered to take him. The other lodger was called Harry. He was almost entirely uncommunicative, and never said more than a word or two at the dinner table. Eventually Alec and the widow took to conducting their conversations as if Harry were not there—occasionally referring to him in the third person, forgetting that he was sitting at the table with them.

"Poor man," she confided to him one evening when Harry had gone off to a function at the returned servicemen's club. "He was a prisoner of the Japs. That's what it did to a lot of them. It broke them. Some managed all right, but others . . ." She left the sentence unfinished.

He nodded. He understood. She had had a number of ex-servicemen as lodgers, she had told him; she knew about them and what they had been through.

"Not that he might have had all that much to say anyway," she said. "Some men are like that, aren't they? People think that they're keeping it all inside them, but there really isn't very much there in the first place. And women, too, of course—I wouldn't want you to think that I was picking on men."

"No. Of course not."

She warmed to her subject. "It's just that women can talk about their feelings. You know that, don't you? They can tell other women what they're worried about. They can speak about it. And that makes it much easier for them."

She looked at him, and he thought that perhaps she was wondering what his feelings were, and this made him ask himself whether he should have more feelings than he did. It had never occurred to him to think too much about how he felt about things. You didn't do that, did you? Not if you were Scottish. If you were Scottish you just got on with it—you did what you had to do and you didn't complain about things or analyse them too much. What possible good did that do?

Then one evening Harry knocked on his door and asked if he could have a chat.

"Just a short chat, mate," he said. "You don't mind, do you? Sometimes a fellow needs to talk."

Alec assured him that he did not mind. He ushered him into the room and offered him the sole chair while he sat on the bed. "Not much good for entertaining," he said. "But it's quiet round here and Joan does her best for us."

"Too true," said Harry. "She's a good woman."

There was a brief silence. Then Harry asked Alec how old he was.

"Just twenty. Last week was my twentieth birthday."

Harry reached out to shake his hand. "Sorry, I didn't know it was your birthday. But many happy whatnots and so on. Good on you."

Alec thanked him. The silence returned.

Then Harry said, "I'm thirty-two meself." He paused. "Had my thirtieth birthday in . . . in the place they kept us. The Japs. The camp."

Alec looked down at the floor. "It must have been bad."

Harry's eyes widened. "Bad? You said bad?"

"Yes. Being a prisoner . . ."

Harry nodded. "It was very bad all right. That's why I don't speak about it very much."

Alec understood. "That's natural. And you don't have to."

"Except sometimes I want to, you know. Sometimes I feel I need to tell somebody about what happened."

There was a short silence. Then Alec said, "Your mates? The ones who were with you in the camp? Can you speak to them?"

Harry looked down at the floor. "Not all of them made it . . ."

"I'm sorry."

"My best mate copped it. If he were here, then I'd

speak to him. But he's not." A pause. "Dysentery. Or that's what got him finally. A lot of things before that. Then you get something that finishes you off. Sometimes that was just the sun. As simple as that. The sun."

Alec said nothing. He was trying to think of people he had known who had died, and the sudden realisation came that there was nobody—or nobody very close. A boy at school died of tuberculosis, but he had not known him very well. An aunt had died, but she lived up in Shetland and he had only seen her once or twice. How old did you have to be before you got to know death?

"I almost got it. Almost," Harry continued. "There was a guard we were all dead frightened of. He was a short man—big stomach—and we were all walking skeletons, you know; rib cages, shoulders, all these bones you didn't know you had until the Japs got you and you started to starve.

"This man called me out of the parade one morning and started bawling his head off at me. I had no idea why he chose me—I hadn't done anything—I was just standing there. Just like this; trying to keep upright. If you fell over they could punish you for it, and so we all tried to keep standing.

"This man pulled me out in front of all the other fellows and was yelling away in Japanese before he took a stick from one of the other Japs and started to beat me. My mates said he beat me in front of everyone for about five minutes. Then the stick breaks, and he throws the pieces down. One of them hit my ear and made a gash in it. See? Look at it here. Just a little scar, but I got it the same time that I got all the big ones on my back.

"I never worked out why he chose me. One of the officers said it had nothing to do with me, that it wasn't personal. He just wanted to beat somebody."

Alec looked up at him. "I'm really sorry to hear this," he said.

Harry looked embarrassed. "I shouldn't have told you, mate. I'm sorry. I shouldn't have made you listen to all that."

"No, of course you should have told me."

Harry closed his eyes. "I'm still frightened, you know. Every day. I'm terrified. I wake up terrified. I go to bed terrified. The war's over, but not in my head, Alec—things stop in the outside world, you know, but they carry on in people's heads."

KAY COULD SEE THAT DAVID WANTED TO SAY something. She waited for him.

"I've often thought about that," he said. "I have a friend who's a psychologist. She deals with people who have gone through traumatic events."

"Post-traumatic stress syndrome," said Andrew. "My father talked to me about that. He helped lifeboat crews sometimes. He said some of them went to pieces after they had pulled somebody out of the water—a body, that is. He said they could have nightmares."

David nodded. "Who doesn't?"

"Have nightmares?" asked Hugh.

"Yes."

Hugh shook his head. "I don't."

"You don't remember them. You probably have them."

"I don't think so."

David turned back to Kay. "There are different views of all this, you know. There are people—psychologists and psychiatrists—who say that you should talk about traumatic experiences. Others say you shouldn't—you should try to forget. You should just get on with your life, not dwell on what happened."

She smiled. "You mean the 'pull your socks up' school?"

"Yes."

She looked thoughtful. "Do you think that pulling your socks up, whistling a cheerful tune—that sort of thing—ever worked? Or did it just bury things for the time being? Put them away until they resurfaced later?"

"How did people get through the Second World War? They helped one another. They sang. They gritted their teeth. I don't think they had therapists to help them."

Kay looked out of the window. Was this the same country they were travelling through? The country that sang and gritted its teeth and accepted its tiny rations? That drank tea while bombs rained down and sent its young men up into aerial combat after a few hours of learning how to fly? The same place?

AFTER HE HAD BEEN WITH HER FOR A YEAR, the widow said coyly: "You need to meet somebody, Alec. A fine boy like you should have a girl, and there are plenty of girls around who would jump at the chance of somebody like you. You don't think so? Come on, Alec, it's true, you know. Lots of young men have this odd notion that there's nobody ever going to look twice at them, but they're wrong, you know."

He laughed at this. "Me, Mrs. Thomas? What do I want to get married for?"

She blushed. "Men have certain needs, Alec."

He laughed again. "I'm fine as I am, Mrs. Thomas. Maybe some time in the future, but for now I'm happy by myself."

She became brisk. "Well, you just let me know when you want me to introduce you to somebody and I can arrange it. There's that girl down the way there—you know that man who owns the garage? Those people. Their daughter. You've seen her, I should imagine. There's her for starters. You could get your knees under the table with them, I think."

He nodded, and the subject was dropped. He enjoyed female company, but he lacked the confidence to do anything about it. And he thought, anyway, that his life was full enough as it was. He had a warehouse job with a company that imported and sold agricultural machinery and it kept him busy. At the end of each day he found that he lacked the energy to go out very much, although he occasionally joined friends from work to go to the pub. He found it difficult, though, to join in their banter. They had spent their whole lives in Fremantle or Perth and he knew none of the characters or incidents they talked about. Who was Eddie Pencey, and why was he so funny? What exactly had Bill O'Connor done that landed him in trouble with Old Man Harris? Why was Mavis Edwards implacably angry with her brother's friend?

Homesickness, too, played its part. Every two weeks there was a letter from his mother. She wrote several pages, on plain paper on which she had drawn the pencil lines herself. She told him of the latest doings of his younger brothers. Jack had been in a fight and had a cut above his left eye. It was that same boy who had done it; he was trouble, that Maclaren boy, and would go too far one of these days. Jack said it wasn't his fault, and she believed him, but he should learn to stay away from situations in which that sort of thing happened.

He sent her money, and she always acknowledged the postal orders and told him what she had used the money for. There had been new shoes for both of the younger boys—they would be writing to him to thank him, she said. They never did.

Money was tight at home, but there were signs that things were getting better. Some food was coming off the ration and that made a difference. There were signs that summer would be warm this year, which was a blessing, although she could imagine how hot it must be out there for him and how he might be pleased to get a bit of Scotland's cool weather for a change.

He read each of her letters several times, folding them carefully and putting them back in their envelopes. People kept letters then, filing them away in shoe boxes or drawers, tying them in bundles with string or tape. Whole lives had their record in those bundles, which might be kept until well after anybody remembered who the correspondents were. He put her letters in the suitcase he kept on top of his wardrobe. He marked each envelope with the date that it had been received, so that he could keep track of the time taken by the mail-boats to complete the journey. Scotland was so far away: thirty-six days on the mail-boats, although there was talk of that coming down by a week. He would never see it again—he was sure of that. This was his home now, this vast land with singing empty skies and its impossible distances. This was his landscape: this expanse of ochres and reds, of dust and rock and eucalyptus-scented forests. In this emptiness he must find his place, and somebody who might share it with him.

AFTER THREE YEARS IN FREMANTLE HE WAS approached by a man in a bar who said to him that he worked on the railway in South Australia. They were looking for men, he said, and the opportunities were good.

"The pay's better than what you're getting—I guarantee that. Holidays good too. Three weeks in your first year; four in the second. Then you get a long leave every other year: two months. That's because you have to be prepared to live in places where there's not much going on. But so what? Who cares what's going on—I don't.

"Here's the address. You write to this Mr. Tomlinson, see, and you tell him what you've been doing—don't bother to give too much detail—he just wants to know that you're not the sort who goes from job to job every few months. This isn't work for somebody who wants to flit about. This is work for men who want a career. There's a difference, you know. Two different sorts of men: those who are never going to settle to anything, and those who want a career. Chalk and cheese, if you ask me."

He took the piece of paper with Mr. Tomlinson's address on it and he wrote to him that same evening. He wanted a change from what he was doing. There was no chance of promotion in the company for which he worked, and he did not particularly like his immediate boss, a mean-spirited man with a pencil-thin moustache who enjoyed finding fault with his work, no matter how hard he tried. He would hand in his notice and go to South Australia.

The widow said: "Oh, Alec, how am I going to get

by without you? No, I shouldn't say that. I shouldn't stand in your way. But you've been a bit of a son to me these last couple of years, and when you've been by yourself you appreciate having somebody about the place. Oh dear, I'm going to start crying at this rate and I shouldn't because this is a big opportunity for you and you must always seize opportunities with both hands. With both hands."

He bought her a present of a bowl, which he wrapped carefully and presented on the morning of his departure.

"It's French, I think," he said. "Least, that's what the lady who sold it to me said. She said this was a French bowl."

"French! Oh, Alec, you honey, I'm going to treasure this, you know. It's going straight in the cabinet, make no mistake about that."

She saw him off on the train. She stood on the platform and waved as the train pulled out. He would never see her again, he knew that, and was silent as the train drew out of the station and started its long haul across the wheat-belt of Western Australia to Kalgoorlie and the wastes of the Nullarbor Plain beyond.

19

HE KNEW IMMEDIATELY THAT THE DECISION to take the job in Adelaide was the right one. The railway provided him with a single-bedroomed flat of his own and gave him a job in the freight office. For the first time he had real responsibility, and he responded well to the trust. The people with whom he worked were friendly, and he realised that he was becoming part of a family of railway workers. "It's not like other jobs," one of them said to him. "With other jobs, you're an employee—you work for somebody. On the railway, you're a member of a family. And the family will see you right, you know. You play fair with the family and the family plays fair with you."

He now felt more at home. He thought of Scotland less frequently, and gradually the memories of Ayrshire started to fade. In his dreams, he noticed, though, he might still be back in Scotland more often than he was in Australia. On occasion, the setting of a dream was in a world that was half Scotland and half Australia: a street might be a street from his home town in Ayrshire, built of Scottish stone and washed by Scottish rain, but it might turn a corner and become quite suddenly a dry plain dotted with houses with red tin roofs.

He began to understand what it was that held this new society together. He appreciated the rough equality, the resolute cheerfulness, the attitude of dogged acceptance of the harshness of nature, of dust, of flies, of drought. Scotland was soft and feminine: all greenery and diffused light; Australia was stark, the sun chiselling out hard contrasts of light and shade. Scotland was forgiving; Australia was uncompromising, and yet everywhere there was a sense of being untrammelled, unconstrained. Nobody could tell you what to do in Australia. Nobody was better than the next man down under. Or so the official version went. Of course there were the blackfellers, as his workmates called them, and he was still enough of a Scot to feel for them in their plight. "It's not right," he wrote home. "I can't tell you all that much about it, but I just feel it's not right. And nobody wants to talk about it because they don't see anything wrong in it. But it is wrong, isn't it? Robert Burns would have said that it's wrong, wouldn't he?"

He worked in Adelaide for three years before the railway said that he could now be offered a siding of his own. "In the Outback, of course, you understand," his supervisor explained. "But it'll be your own show and you'll be in charge of a lot of track. Give me your decision by next week."

It did not take him that long. “I’ll take it,” he said.

“Good. It’s not everyone who can do that sort of job, but we think that you’ve got what it takes, even if you’re still a bit young.”

He was twenty-five.

The supervisor looked at him thoughtfully. “You’ll need a wife,” he said. “Do you want to pick one up before you go, or wait until you’re there? The advantage of getting one out there is that she’ll know what it’s like. It’s when they don’t know what it’s like that you run into trouble.”

“It can wait,” he said.

The supervisor nodded. “Fine. But remember that any honeymoon is going to have to depend on our having somebody to relieve you for the duration. So the job comes first, understand. Then the honeymoon.”

ANDREW LOOKED INCREDULOUS. WHAT DID people marry for in those days? To have somebody to cook for them, if they were men? To have somebody to pay the bills, if they were women? Bizarre. It was so different now. You married for love. You married because it was comfortable for two people to live together—on terms of equality—and share everything. Of course they didn’t have the internet then and you had to go off somewhere to meet people. You had to write to them. How strange life must have been. Unwired. Cut off. Lonely. Off-line.

There would never be loneliness again, he thought—it was simply unnecessary. We had eradicated smallpox and polio and a whole lot of other diseases, and now we were eradicating loneliness. Except that was simply not true. The more we spoke to one another electronically, the more information we bombarded one another with, the easier we made it to move from place to place—vast distances sometimes—the more detached from one another we seemed to become. Loneliness had a long future ahead of it, after all.

HIS SIDING WAS ON THE GHAN LINE THAT IN those days went from Adelaide in South Australia up as far as Alice Springs in the Northern Territory. Hope Springs was not far from a point of confluence of two major Outback tracks—rough dirt roads that were the only route through the vast dry plains of the continent's parched heart. The Oodnadatta Track came down from the north-west, skirting the western side of Lake Eyre, while the Birdsville Track struck north-east towards Southern Queensland. These roads could trap cars in sand or, if it rained, in mud. Great ingenuity was required to get out once trapped, and people could be stuck for days. Travellers also had to stick carefully to the track; any straying off the route was potentially fatal; a wrong turning, a loss of a reference point, and one would quickly perish under the unrelenting sun. Tales were common of cars and trucks being found just a few hundred yards off the track, their drivers dead from thirst and heat; told to warn people of the dangers of thinking they could flout the rules of survival in the Outback. "A few hours and it'll have you," people said. "Just a few hours is all you've got."

The pastoral properties scattered along these tracks were immense. It was common for one house to preside over a stretch of land that ran fifty or sixty miles across. Such land supported cattle, but only just, and each animal needed a vast area of grazing to survive. Here and there, marked by patches of green in the predominantly brown landscape, artesian springs brought water to the surface, allowing the cattle and dingoes to slake their thirst.

There were occasional isolated towns—collections of simple houses, a country pub and store, a police post. Then there were the sidings, which were one step down from the towns. These consisted of a railway office, a water tower for the replenishing of the steam locomotives, a station-master's house and a bunkhouse for railway staff passing through. The bunkhouse might also be used for people from the big cattle stations who might for some reason arrive to catch a train a day before it was due in. It might also occasionally shelter the men who drifted through the Outback in search of work: stockmen or shearers, mechanics, men who had tried everything else and who were now prepared to take on any job in the most inhospitable of surroundings.

Hope Springs had the benefit of ample water. There was an old well, dug in the eighteen-nineties, not far from the railway siding, and a rough bathing pool had been fashioned out of railway sleepers. The water, he had been told, was ancient water—it had fallen tens of thousands of years ago in the wet north of Australia and had percolated down over time into the vast reservoir that lay beneath the central Australian depression. It would never dry up; it would always force its way to just below the surface, and once pumped up it would quickly evaporate in the glare of the sun. But not before some of it had been piped to the station-master's house and to the high tank from which the dangling canvas elephant's trunk filled the engines.

The previous station-master was retiring. He and his wife had been there for eighteen years and were going back to the small town on the coast from which they had come. Their time in the Outback was written on their faces—in the lines, the texture of the skin, in the weathered look that came from all that time in an atmosphere of dryness and baking heat.

They were hospitable in the week they spent together on the hand-over. The down train would take their effects away just as the up train had brought his. He helped them pack it into the wagons—the standing lamps, the Morris chairs, the photographs in their frames, wrapped in several thicknesses of brown paper, the bed-linen tied in bundles. His baggage was simpler: several suitcases of clothing, some kitchen items, his small collection of books. "A bachelor's possessions," the station-master's wife said, smiling.

They left, and he was in control of the siding. It would be two days before the next train came, and so he busied himself with such paperwork as the job entailed. He waited for somebody to come along the track and call in for water, but on that first day there was nobody. He retired that night and looked out of the window of the bedroom from his bed, up at a sky that was almost white with stars. He got up and went onto the veranda, where it was cooler. Looking south, he saw the Southern Cross, suspended in the velvet sky. It gave him comfort, located him in this vast emptiness. At least there would be other human eyes that were looking up at that at that precise moment.

He thought: I shall not be able to bear this loneliness. I should have stayed in Adelaide; I should not have come out here. I should not have done this.

A YEAR AFTER HIS APPOINTMENT AS STATION-master at Hope Springs, he took his first annual leave of three weeks and travelled to Sydney. The rail journey there was not a quick one, and precious days of holiday were spent on it, but he had never seen Sydney and was keen to do so. There was another reason, too, why he wanted to go there: his pen-friend lived in the city and after six months of correspondence he had suggested they meet.

He had started writing to her on a whim. One of the passengers on the up train to Alice Springs had come into his office during a stop and asked to send a telegram. This was something he could do, sending the message down the wire that followed the line back to Adelaide. He enjoyed sending telegrams, in fact, as it provided some variety in his work and the messages often amused him. HAVE CHANGED MY MIND was a message that he had been asked to send on more than one occasion; a long train journey is a time for reflection, perhaps, and the mind might easily change in such circumstances. Another simply read, FORGIVEN STOP COMPLETELY STOP, while, in contrast, yet another had said THIS IS WAR. He had the power to decline messages of a hostile or improper nature and had hesitated on this wording; forgiveness was one thing, war another, but he eventually let it through. WILL YOU MARRY ME? had at least the attraction of simplicity and unambiguity, and he hoped that the answer might be yes. On rare occasions, he received telegrams to await passengers passing through in either direction and had once received a telegram that read YES STOP. He had delivered that without any indication of having read the message—the rules stated that you were not to pay attention to or use what was said in any telegram—but he had tried to work out, from the reaction of the recipient, what the question had been. He had been a man in his mid-forties somewhere and he had opened the envelope and read the telegram without giving anything away—at least at first. Then he had stared glumly out of the window and Alec had understood that yes could be bad news as easily as it could be good.

The passenger who asked to send a telegram that day was a mining engineer. He had something technical to say in his message—something to do with ore samples—but he had stayed for a chat and had left behind a week-old copy of the **Sydney Morning Herald**. "Stale news, I'm afraid, but there's a bit in there about the cricket that you may like to read."

He had thanked him and set the paper to the side. That evening he had read it from cover to cover, including the advertisements. One had been for an agency that provided pen-friends; for a small fee one would be given the names of up to three people who were keen to exchange letters with you—every one of them screened for suitability, the advertisers claimed. On impulse he had written a request for a woman correspondent between twenty and twenty-five, living anywhere in Australia. He almost did not post the letter, but remembered just in time to give it to the driver of the next train down to Adelaide.

He was sent the name of a young woman called Alison Morsby, who lived just outside Sydney. She was interested in the cinema, dancing and flowers. She also read the novels of Nevil Shute, her profile revealed, and Charles Dickens. She was not very good at tennis, but she liked swimming.

He thought about this. There was no cinema there, of course, and no dancing, except for the annual ball held at another siding sixty miles away. That attracted every bachelor and spinster within a radius of several hundred miles, but was more about drinking, he had heard, than dancing. There were flowers, of course, but only for a brief spell in the year, and they had to be resistant to the harsh climate of the Outback. There was no tennis, and the only swimming was in the water hole at the spring, where there was room for one or two strokes in the tank made of old railway sleepers. He had heard about Nevil Shute's **A Town Like Alice**—everybody had, as it had just been published and was much discussed in the papers; he could talk about that, he supposed, even if he had not yet read it. But Charles Dickens was another matter.

He wrote a brief and rather formal letter, introducing himself. He wondered whether he should send a picture, but decided against it. He was not sure about the etiquette of that, and felt that it would be better to wait. If a correspondence developed, then pictures could be exchanged.

Her reply came rather more quickly than he had expected. She had been very pleased to get his letter, she wrote. She enjoyed getting letters and had been writing for two years to a pen-friend in England, a young woman of her own age, whose dream it was to come to Australia one day. This young woman worked in a shop in Bournemouth, but was planning to move to London when she had saved up enough to do so. "I really like getting her letters and hearing about her life, which is very different from the life I lead in Paramatta. I have never worked in a shop, but I have a job as a secretary in a municipal office. I type the reports that building inspectors make when they go to inspect new houses. They look at the foundations etc. and have to check that everything meets the right standards. You'd be surprised, you really would, by some of the things that builders try to get away with. Sometimes I can hardly believe what the inspectors say about builders' tricks."

He wrote back the day he received her letter. He told her about his job and about his time in Fremantle. He said that he was thinking of getting a ham radio operator's licence, as it would be useful to talk to people all over the place. He said that he had heard ham radio enthusiasts sent each other cards after their contacts and that some people had thousands of these cards, from places as far off as Russia. "I think they keep a close eye on radio sets in Russia," he wrote.

She sent him cuttings from a newspaper feature called "Cooking Tips for Blokes." This was for bachelors who had to cook for themselves, and it gave instructions on the preparation of simple dishes, **suitable for men**. "I know that some men are quite good cooks," she wrote, "but a lot of them aren't. My brother, Russell, can hardly boil an egg! I had to show him! I'm not exaggerating."

He wrote back: "Thanks a lot for 'Cooking Tips for Blokes.' It looks like an excellent series and I look forward to the next one. I tried that recipe for soda bread and I think it was okay, but the bread was a bit heavy. Do you think they left something out when they printed the recipe? Don't you have to have yeast to make bread?"

She replied to his question with another recipe for ordinary bread, and he reported success with that. "I wouldn't have to go to the bakery any more," he wrote, "if there was one here, which there isn't. In fact, the nearest proper store is at Marree, which is eighty-three miles away."

He wondered whether this picture of his life

would put her off. If you lived where she did, you could get into the city in no time at all. You could go to dances and to the beach. You could read the newspapers on the day they were printed. You could buy fresh bread baked by other people.

But she gave no sign of thinking that his life was difficult or dull. "It must be very nice to have the time to sit and think," she wrote. "I seem to have no time and often ask myself: Where has the day gone? I envy you having time to look about you and to think about things."

Emboldened, he wrote, "One of these days you should come and see this place. You might even like it! Who knows?"

To which she replied: "I'd love to come out there some time. I've never been to the Outback, but of course I've seen plenty of pictures of it. But pictures don't show the wind, do they? Or the smell of the trees and shrubs."

He thought: No, they don't. And he went outside and closed his eyes and took a deep breath of the wind from the north, which was a dry wind that carried the smell of emptiness upon it, and of the trees that clustered around the water hole, and of the salt pans beyond that, white, shimmering, brittle under the sun.

WHILE HE WAS IN SYDNEY HE STAYED IN A small hotel in the Rocks. The hotel had a bar that sold the beer brewed in the brewery next door, and a rather dingy dining room that claimed on the menu to be "one of Sydney's most highly regarded dining experiences." The menu, though, did not seem to support this. Brown Windsor Soup was the only choice of first course, and for the second one could choose macaroni cheese, Irish stew or baked fish.

They had exchanged photographs by now, and so he had no difficulty in recognising her. He felt, though, that she was markedly more attractive than she had appeared in the picture she had sent him; it was something to do with her eyes, he thought; there was a quality in them that drew him in. He was nervous. He had never been much good with attractive women; he was convinced that any woman like that would be bound to find somebody else more exciting than he was, and that made him hold back. He could not imagine that any woman, let alone an attractive one, could fall in love with him. After all, who was he? He was a Scotsman who worked for the railways in a very remote spot. He had nothing to offer anybody—no money, no experience of the world, no dashing good looks.

She said to him: "You're just as I imagined you. Thanks for being the same as you are in your letters."

This took him by surprise. "And you," he stuttered. "You're even better."

He showed her the menu. "It says that they're pretty good. I thought it was just an ordinary hotel, but you see what it says? One of Sydney's most highly regarded dining experiences. See it there?"

"Sometimes the really good places are very straightforward," she said. "They don't have to be flashy." She ran her eye down the menu. "Macaroni cheese. One of my favourites. I think there was a recipe for that in 'Cooking Tips for Blokes,' wasn't there?"

He remembered it well. "I tried that one. I make it once a week, sometimes more."

"It must be hard for you," she said. "Having to do all your own cooking like that. And run a railway siding. I don't know how you do it."

There was silence. In that moment, both of them understood what the purpose of this meeting was and how it would end.

HE PROPOSED TO HER FOUR DAYS LATER, IN A café beside the cinema in which they had just seen a film together. He said, "I know this is a bit sudden—I know that. But I can't bear the thought of going back without saying something that I've been trying to pluck up the courage to say for a long time."

She looked down at the blue gingham tablecloth. He swallowed.

"So what I really want to ask you is this: Will you marry me? I know that I haven't got much to offer and that you're probably going to turn me down, and I hope that you're not angry at me for asking . . ."

"No."

He caught his breath. Of course she would turn him down; of course she would.

"I mean no, I'm not angry with you; how could I be? And the answer to your question is yes, of course I'll marry you, Alec. I've been hoping you'd ask me and I . . . well, I couldn't bear it either if you went back to Hope Springs without asking me. So the answer is yes."

He reached across the table and took her hand. "I think you can get a special licence if you have to go off somewhere like the Outback. You don't have to give the same period of notice, you know, the banns . . ."

"I've heard that too," she said.

"Of course I'll have to ask your father."

She shook her head. "He's dead. Italy. When they went across to Sicily and there was this big battle . . ."

"Of course. Your mother then."

She smiled. "She'll say yes. She's been getting at me to get married for ages."

ANDREW SMILED. "IT WAS SO DIFFERENT then, wasn't it?"

"Yes, it was," said Kay. "People were more formal in the way they spoke to one another."

He shook his head. "That's not what I meant. I meant marriage—they made a bigger thing of it."

"And you don't?"

He thought for a moment. "Well, maybe . . . But anyway: there she was, happy to go off to a place where she'd have nothing to do, no company, apart from her husband . . . Who'd do that today?"

21

"I'M GOING TO PLANT FLOWERS."

She was standing on the back veranda of the house at Hope Springs, looking out at the line of casuarina trees that provided some shelter for the house from the north.

"Where? Near the trees?"

"Yes. In between them, and maybe in a bed between this veranda and the water tank. Over there. What do you think?"

"I would like flowers. Roses maybe."

"I'm not sure how roses would do. We could try, though. I thought, maybe, we could find some of the flowers that seem to like these dry conditions."

He said that he thought that would be sensible. For a brief period in the spring, the Outback blossomed, and there were wide expanses of native flowers, painting the land with yellow, blue, red.

"There's plenty of water," he said. "At least there's plenty right here."

She had plants and seeds sent up from Adelaide, and brought them on in a nursery she had created on the shady side of the house. He found it astonishing that the earth could be so bountiful in the face of all that dryness and dust, but she pointed out that it was always possible to create small corners of growth in the most unlikely of conditions.

And she began to transform the house as well. The bare rooms of the station-master's house saw the introduction of rugs and curtains. She painted the walls herself, and hung on them pictures and decorative china plates.

He marvelled at the change. "I would never have imagined you could do so much with a place like this," he complimented her. "Look at it!"

She took satisfaction in his approbation. "It's our home, Alec. I want it to be something special."

The garden became steadily larger. With the area immediately about the house now cultivated, she turned her attention to the ground around the siding platform itself. The name **Hope Springs** was spelled out in Namaqualand daisies and hardy thyme plants, and behind there was a rose bed. When the Alice Springs train stopped, the passengers got off and walked around the flower beds. Many of them took photographs of the **Hope Springs** floral sign, posing in front of it.

There was a bed that she cultivated specially for passengers to pick a flower from to take with them when they boarded the train again. She received many compliments, some of which were written in a visitors' book that she placed on a table in front of the office.

"You've certainly made the desert bloom," was the most common remark that people made.

"I cried," wrote one. "Why don't more people do this? Why don't more people bother to create beauty like you do?"

A subsequent visitor had pencilled in an answer. "Because they don't care," he, or she, wrote. "That's why."

SHE BECAME PREGNANT, ALTHOUGH IT WAS four years before this happened. By then they had almost given up hope, and she hardly dared believe it when, on a visit to the clinic in the nearest town, this was confirmed.

"You should go down to Adelaide," said the doctor. "Anything could happen out there and if it did . . . well, I don't see what could be done."

She reluctantly agreed, and a few weeks later she made the journey on the down train from Alice. He installed her in her compartment and they kissed before he left the carriage.

"You'll have to go now," she said. "I'll write the moment we get there."

"The train can't go until I blow my whistle," he said. "We have all the time in the world."

"No," she said. "We don't."

"Don't speak like that," he said.

He got off the train and it began to move. She leaned out of the window, waving until he was out of sight and she could no longer see the colourful floral sign, nor the roses, nor the casuarina trees.

In Adelaide she stayed with a distant cousin of her mother's. This woman was pleased to have the company, and was almost too solicitous in looking after her. It was a relief when, after the birth of their daughter, she was able to go home again.

"I'm happier than I can possibly say," he remarked, as he rocked the infant in his arms. "You, me and the baby."

"In our home," she said.

"Yes, in our home."

He looked down at the child and touched her forehead gently with the tip of a finger. "Bless you," he said. "Bless you, little darling."

She watched this. She loved the sight of gentleness in men. Why were they so reluctant to show this side of their nature, she wondered. Why did they have to be so tough, so in command of everything, so indifferent to the feelings that they must have, somewhere beneath that hard exterior of theirs?

The baby, this tiny girl, was the woman in the train, making the journey from Scotland so many years later. Kay thought of her parents and of what they had been through. She thought of Hope Springs, which she had visited once as an adult, just to see whether the memories of childhood were accurate. There was a floral sign, was there not? She found the place where it had been. She found the rose beds behind the house. It was just as she remembered it, except it was somehow smaller. The world is like that; memory has the effect of a telescope, making bigger the things we see through its lens, making them bigger than they really are.

She stood at the side of the flower beds that her mother had laid out and spent so much time working on. Their shapes were clear enough, but they were now merely shapes of bare earth, like skeletons entombed just below the surface of the ground. We change the earth and our changes may only be temporary; yet the signs of what we have done may persist, as these mounds did.

HUGH LISTENED TO HER ACCOUNT OF HER parents' life and thought: Yes, there are people for whom love, like everything else in their lives, happens slowly. He thought, too, of moral luck.

"Moral luck."

Kay looked at him enquiringly.

"What exactly is moral luck?"

Hugh smiled. "I only know what it means because I took a philosophy course at university; I had a gap to fill in, and I chose philosophy. We had a lecturer who was interested in moral luck and started to talk about it one day. He talked for a full hour. It had nothing to do with what we were meant to be studying, but we sat there transfixed as he explained what was meant by moral luck."

"Which is what?"

"It's not quite the same thing as fate, or chance, even if fate and chance play a part in it." He paused. They were all looking at him now: David, Kay, Andrew.

"Shall I give you an example?"

Kay nodded. "Yes."

"Okay. There are two people: let's call them Tom and Dick."

"What happened to Harry?"

"He's not in this example. He doesn't matter. The point is this: Tom's parents are nice people. They provide him with a good example and bring him up to help others and so on. Tom does well at school and gets a good job. Everything goes well for him. Now, on to poor Dick. Dick's parents are dishonest. His father is violent and is in and out of prison; his mother drinks, shall we say. Maybe she sleeps around too. Dick gets into trouble himself when he's sixteen and ends up being sent to reform school. Tom has good moral luck, Dick has bad."

They thought about it in silence.

"So . . ."

"The fact that Tom did well and stayed out of trouble is due to his good luck in being born to his particular parents. That was luck, and it had a big effect on how he led his life. Dick may not have been any worse a person inside—he may have had the capacity to be better than he was, but his bad moral luck meant that he was never able to develop any of that." He paused. "Have you seen those photographs of war crimes trials? You see the judges sitting in a row and then the witnesses—the victims, or relatives of the victims—and then you see the prisoners on trial. Luck determines that the victims are on the right side of the barrier and the perpetrators on the wrong. Both could equally well have done or received what was done or received. Both would have been capable of it, had their moral luck been different and had they found themselves in the others' shoes. So what happens to you in this life, particularly whether you are good or bad, is largely dependent on factors beyond your control—in other words, on the sort of luck you have."

"We aren't responsible for our characters?" asked David.

"No."

Kay frowned. "Really? Do you really think it's that arbitrary?"

Hugh did.

"But we can decide to lead better lives. We can decide to make something of ourselves—surely that must be possible."

David intervened. "I see his point. There may be some room for us to change things for the better, but that depends on our having the luck to see the possibility of improvement. We might not have that luck and so we may never know that there's something we can do—or **should** do, for that matter."

"Everything's a matter of luck," said Kay. "Our whole lives are affected by it—everything."

Kay thought: The newspaper, the **Sydney Morning Herald**—it was luck, pure luck, that my father read the advertisement that day. And it was luck too that he happened to see **Men needed for Western Australia**. Luck.

The thought that went through David's mind

was of a dropped oar. Had he not dropped that oar in that particular river at that particular time, then his life would have been different.

"In my case," said Hugh, "everything depended on getting off a train at the wrong station. It all flowed from that."

23

"THERE ARE VARIOUS WAYS IN WHICH YOU can get off at the wrong station. You can . . ."

". . . go to sleep," said Kay. "That happened to me once. I went to sleep and when I awoke I was three stations down the line."

YES, YOU CAN GO TO SLEEP, AND THEN WAKE up and think that the next station is yours when in fact you've just passed it. That's easily done. Or you can misread the sign on the platform. You know how hard it is to make out letters when they're flashing past—well, you might do that. Or you can get on the wrong train in the first place, and then get out at what you think is the right station only to find it's the wrong line.

I was reading at the time. I was sitting there reading a book that was so gripping that I had no idea where we were. Then, as the train drew into a station, I looked out of the window and saw a building that I thought I recognised. My destination was a town in the west of England—not an important place, but the company I worked for had clients there and I went there from time to time to deal with their issues, travelling all the way down from Edinburgh to London and then across England.

I closed my book, stood up and took my overnight case from the rack above my seat. Had I looked out of the window at that point I would have seen that I was at the wrong station, but I did not. Even so, I might have realised my mistake had I looked about me once I was on the platform, but again I did not. One of my shoelaces was undone, and I reached down to tie it. The lace broke, and so I had to re-thread it so that the remaining bit did the work. That took time, and I was conscious as I did so that the train was pulling out of the station. When I stood up I saw the name of the station staring me in the face.

I felt so foolish. It was not a disaster—my meeting with the clients was not until first thing the following morning, and I knew that I would be able to catch the next train down the line in good time to book into my hotel at my original destination. But it was such an avoidable mistake, and it would mean a wait for an hour or two on an uncomfortable bench.

There was a timetable on a board a few yards away and I went to look at this. There were several later trains, I saw, but the next one would not stop for another couple of hours. I had alighted, it seemed, at a station that was not important enough for each and every train to call at: many went through without stopping.

I looked around for somewhere to sit. There was a bench near the steps that led to a footbridge across the line, but it looked rickety and unappealing. My gaze moved down the platform, and then I saw her. She was standing at the entrance to the platform, looking at her watch, glancing anxiously around. It was immediately obvious why she was there: she had come to meet somebody off the train from which I had alighted, only to discover that she was too late, or had got the wrong train.

There was something about her that drew me to her. She was a complete stranger, but I felt almost as if there was some sort of affinity between us. Without really thinking about it, I started to cross the platform towards her. At first she seemed not to notice me, but then our eyes met. I've often thought about that first exchange of looks. What did she think I was doing?

"You were expecting somebody?"

She hesitated as she weighed whether to rebuff me. Men did not approach women on railway stations; they just did not. Yet normal human courtesy, which is quite capable of surviving social inhibitions, won through. "Yes. But obviously she's not coming. That was the London train, wasn't it?"

"Yes. There were some other people who got off, but I didn't really see them. Perhaps your friend wasn't on it."

She sighed. "I don't think she was. It's infuriating. She's done this before—changed her mind and forgotten to tell me about it. It's really inconsiderate of her."

I commiserated. "Yes, it must be."

"And you?" she asked. "What about you? Going somewhere?"

I shook my head. "I feel a bit stupid. I got off at the wrong station. So now I have to wait here for almost two hours for the next train to where I want to go."

She gave me a sympathetic look. "Bad luck."

I looked at my watch and then spoke on impulse. "It's almost seven," I said. "And I'm hungry. How about dinner?"

She was momentarily taken aback. "Me?"

I gestured to the empty station. "Well, there's nobody else here, as far as I can see. Yes, you. That's a pub over there, isn't it?" I pointed to a building on the other side of the road from the railway station. The Lamb and Flag. There were numerous Lambs and Flags throughout England, and here was one conveniently to hand. "I imagine they do food. How about it?"

She hesitated, but only briefly. "I have to see somebody at nine," she said.

I doubted the truth of this; she needed an excuse to get away if the evening became difficult. "I have to catch my train anyway," I said. "It's at nine-fifteen. We'll have finished by then."

She thought for a moment longer before she said, "Yes, why not?"

We left the station and crossed the road to The Lamb and Flag. "I'm Hugh," I said. "And you're . . ."

"Jenny."

"I'm glad you said we could have dinner. It means I don't have to sit on that platform counting the minutes."

"And I don't have to go back to my place and be cross with my friend."

I remarked that sometimes being stood up could have unexpected benefits, and perhaps this might be such an occasion.

"Maybe," she said. "Maybe."

THE PUB WAS NOT AT ALL BUSY—IT WAS THE evening of an important football match, England against France—and the pub had held out against television. We chose our meal, which was delivered quickly and was piping hot. The conversation was easy, and within a few minutes we found that we each knew rather a lot about one another. She was a teacher, she told me. She originally came from Durham, and had qualified there, but had moved to Gloucestershire a couple of years earlier. She had done so on a whim, and did not regret it. "I think that if you think too much about things, you can end up never doing anything new," she said. "Don't you agree?"

"Such as inviting somebody for dinner two minutes after you've met them?"

She laughed. "Yes, that sort of thing."

She told me that she shared a house in a village with two other teachers, although they all worked at different schools. "We met at an induction weekend," she said. "One of them had already spotted this house, you see, and wanted somebody to share. It's at the end of a long lane. The lane is really rather narrow, and so you have to hope that you don't meet another car when you're driving along it."

"You have to breathe in if you do?"

"More or less. But that hardly ever happens." She paused, looking at me searchingly. "And you? Do you share or . . ."

I noticed her glancing at my hand. You can always tell when somebody is looking for a wedding ring; it's usually obvious enough.

"I share."

She nodded.

"With another chap."

It seemed to me that this was the answer she wanted; or it was the answer she wanted—subject to a qualification.

"The flat's got two bedrooms," I added. "So I decided to share it. It helps with the rent."

She nodded again, and the conversation moved on. She asked me what I was doing on the train, and I explained about my visit to the clients. "They need to have their hands held," I said. "We sell them software, and it's easy enough to use it. They could fix all their problems themselves, but they don't bother. They have to get us to show them how to do it."

"There are children exactly like that," she said. "They need you to show them everything. And then there are ones who don't."

I asked her about the friend she had been expecting. "She's a sort of cousin," she said. "She's a physiotherapist, but she's really scatty. It's always the same. When some guy asks her out, she forgets about everything else. You'd think that she could simply call me on her mobile and tell me. You'd think that, wouldn't you?"

I asked her how we got on before mobile phones were invented. What did people do?

"They wrote letters. They found phone booths."

"It seems so long ago. It seems so impossible."

I looked at my watch. "I mustn't miss the next train."

I was not prepared for what she said next. "You could always come to our place and stay there."

I looked down at the beer I had ordered, unsure as to how to take her remark. Was this that kind of invitation? And if it was, how should I react? She had only known me for a few minutes and she was asking me to stay with her. What sort of person would invite a complete stranger to come home with her? I thought perhaps I had led too sheltered a life.

My surprise had an effect. "Oh, I didn't mean that," she blustered. "I wasn't propositioning you."

This relieved the tension. "I didn't think you were." This, of course, was not strictly true, but I had to say it to spare her feelings.

"We've got a couch," she went on. "It's for visitors."

I took a sip of beer. I did not want to say goodbye to her just yet. "I could stay on the couch," I said. "It would be better than the hotel I'm booked into. I don't like hotels anyway."

"And I could drive you there tomorrow," she offered. "It's the school holidays and I wasn't planning to do anything much."

We were sitting quite close to the bar, and I noticed that the landlord, who had been polishing glasses, had been listening to our conversation. He was smiling, as if to himself, and I knew that he had heard. As I looked in his direction, he gave me a wink. It was a conspiratorial sign, of the sort that one male may exchange with another when one of them has succeeded in the pursuit. I resented this; I wanted to point out to him that the situation was not as he imagined it—I had not been pursuing Jenny. This was simply a friendship. But then I realised that perhaps the wink was capable of another interpretation. Perhaps it was intended to say **I've seen this before.** Perhaps he wanted to say **This is how she operates.**

I looked at her. It was unlikely. It was highly unlikely.

"You don't have to," she said suddenly. "It was just that I didn't want you to feel that you had to catch a train again when you've just got off one."

I smiled at her. "I accept. Thanks very much."

THE NEXT MORNING I TELEPHONED THE CLIents and asked them whether it made much difference to them whether I arrived that or the following day. They replied that it was moderately more convenient to them for it to be the following day, and that settled it. I suggested to Jenny that we go off somewhere and have lunch, and she agreed that this would be a good idea. "And dinner too," I said.

"No, I'll cook for you," she said. "I'll do . . ." She trailed off. "I don't really know what you like. But whatever it is, I'll cook it for you."

"Salmon steaks, salad and new potatoes."

"Exactly what I had in mind," she said.

We had our lunch, and our dinner, and when she ran me to the station the next morning we had already planned for her to come up to Edinburgh, where I lived. It was a long journey, and I wondered about the viability of a long-distance relationship, but we could talk to one another on our computers and in her job she had long holidays. But there was no question in my mind. I had found the right person. This was the woman for me. I was one hundred per cent sure. She was the one.

24

EDINBURGH WAS THE REAL BEGINNING, I suppose. Then there was London, where we went a couple of months ago. And after that there was Paris. By that stage we had decided that I would move to London if I managed to find a suitable job. She could stay where she was, but it would be far easier to see one another when we were separated by a train journey of two hours rather than one of four. Everything was going well—we were completely compatible, as far as I could make out—and we felt quite comfortable in one another's company. The only thing that worried me was what happened in Paris. That was a difficult moment in our relationship. Why? It was all about trust.

Kay sighed. "There was somebody else?"

"There **had been** somebody else . . ."

She sighed again. "Because that's the problem, isn't it? People don't make a clean break. They let things fade away and then, when they take up with somebody else, their ex is still hanging about somewhere, hopeful, perhaps, that things will start again. It gets messy."

"No, it wasn't like that."

She looked surprised. "So what was it like?"

WE STAYED IN A SMALL HOTEL NEAR THE École Militaire. It was not the most obvious part of Paris to stay in for a romantic break like that—it was in a quiet street fairly close to the UNESCO headquarters. Most of the other guests, I think, were there for a UNESCO meeting—something to do with the protection of endangered languages. Some of them seemed to be speaking just such languages, I decided, as I found it difficult even to guess what they were. It's interesting, isn't it, how when you stay in a hotel almost anywhere all you hear are the major languages—Spanish, German, Russian and so on; you very rarely hear anything that sounds utterly foreign. But they were speaking some of those languages in the hotel that weekend—wonderful, exotic languages, including one that had clicks and whistles in it. As it happened, I knew what that was, as I had read about it. It's called !Kung. And it has an exclamation mark in front of it. Imagine talking !English or !French with an exclamation mark. It was lovely to listen to—rather like the sound of the wind in the reeds, or a pair of exotic birds talking to one another on the branch of a tree.

We did all the usual things that visitors to Paris do. I knew the city a bit better than she did, but neither of us was all that familiar with it. We went on the Seine, we spent hours in cafés and restaurants, we walked in gardens. I experienced what I suppose was sheer delight in being there with her. It was one of those times when one is conscious of the fact that there is nowhere else one would wish to be, and nobody else in the world with whom one would prefer to be. I was blissfully happy. Paris makes you feel different. The ordinary you, the you that has to go to work every morning, the you that has to run a household, pay bills, do all of those things—that you is somehow changed into an exciting, artistic, **fully alive** you. That's what Paris does.

I found out all about her. It seemed to both of us to be entirely natural to be sitting in one of the pavement cafés revealing to one another our most intimate thoughts: how we felt about our parents, our brothers and sisters; the things that we liked doing; the books we liked reading; the films we liked. She told me about her life in that town in Gloucestershire and there, in Paris, it seemed somehow exotic, as did my life in Edinburgh.

We arrived late on a Thursday. On Friday we had dinner in a restaurant in the Latin Quarter, one that I had read up about in a guide to Paris that I had brought with me. On Saturday we found another restaurant—one not mentioned in my guide—that seemed even better. And then we returned to the hotel.

I knew immediately that something was wrong when we went into the lobby to get the key to our room. There was a group of people who had just arrived—three men and one woman—and they were in the process of checking in. They must have arrived on a late flight, as their suitcases, still with airline luggage-tags on them, were on the floor beside them.

Jenny had been saying something to me as we stepped through the front door. Then she stopped mid-sentence, staring at the group. I looked at her inquisitively. She had paled and was now half turned away. But she did not do so quickly enough; one of the men in the group had also turned round and seen her. He froze. Then he glanced briefly at me before he turned round again and muttered something to one of his companions.

"What's wrong?"

She ignored my question. "You get the key," she whispered, "I'll see you upstairs." And then she walked very deliberately, with head bowed, through the lobby to the staircase on the other side. I looked back at the group of new arrivals. The man who had looked at us turned his head slightly; he was watching her.

As I waited to collect our key, they were completing their registration. I stole a few glances at the other man, and I think he did the same for me. He was about my age, I think—thirty-ish—and was of similar build. He had blond hair and one of those faces that one sees in northern European countries, including England—a rather ruddy, open, well-fed look. It's not Viking—it's more the sort of look that one finds, say, in the Netherlands. Remember pictures of Dutch boys on packs of butter? That look. I did not like him. I could not put my finger on it, of course, but I think I would have felt uncomfortable in his presence even if he had not caused that reaction in Jenny. They obviously knew one another, and it was equally obvious that there was something between them.

I collected our key and made my way up to the second floor, where Jenny was waiting in the corridor.

"What was all that about?" I asked as I approached her.

She gestured to the door. "Let's talk inside."

I fumbled with the key but eventually succeeded in opening the door. Once inside, I turned to her expectantly. "Well? That guy?"

She took off her coat and threw it down on the bed. "He's called Johnny Bates."

"You know him? Well, obviously you do." I did not intend it, but I think I sounded sarcastic.

She turned to me with a look of appeal. "Yes, I do."

I softened, realising that I was not being sufficiently tactful. She had told me that she had broken up with somebody six months ago and it had not been amicable. It must have been with Johnny Bates.

I made my apology. "Look, Jenny, I'm sorry. It must be awkward for you. Johnny Bates was the person you were involved with. I should have put two and two together."

"Yes, he was."

I tried to make light of the situation. "And now he's here. We go away for a romantic week-end in Paris, and we end up staying in the same hotel as Johnny Bates."

She began to recover. She smiled. "We were here first. He ended up staying in the same hotel as us."

"In that case," I said, "let's forget all about him. No more Johnny Bates."

She put her arms about me. "Good idea," she said.

25

WE WERE DELIBERATELY LATE GOING DOWN for breakfast the following morning. Neither of us said anything about it, but I think we both wanted to make sure that we would not run into Johnny Bates and his party. We succeeded; we were the only people in the dining room and the staff began to clear the other tables while we were still there. Nothing was said about the previous evening's awkward encounter, and I was optimistic that it could be completely forgotten. We were going to be out of the hotel for the rest of the day and we were having dinner in a restaurant. On the following morning—Monday morning—we were going to be leaving for the airport at five in the morning, which meant that we were fairly unlikely to run into Johnny Bates again.

But I was wrong. After we set out that morning, I discovered that I had left my guidebook in the room. We had not walked more than a couple of blocks from the hotel, but I suggested that I could go back and fetch it while Jenny did some window-shopping. She agreed, and I walked briskly back to the hotel and made my way up the small, winding staircase at the back of the lobby. The hotel had a lift—an ancient, cage-like apparatus—but this was so slow, and so cramped, that it was far easier to use the stairs.

I bounded up and more or less collided with Johnny Bates, who was coming down. The stairs were narrow and we could not pass one another; we were face-to-face.

I muttered an apology and started to make my way down to the floor below.

"Listen," he said. "Don't rush off."

I turned back to face him. "Yes?"

"I saw that you were with Jenny. Are you . . ."

I decided to make it easier for him. "Yes, we're going out together."

He seemed to chew on this information. "I see."

I wanted to end the encounter. "I know you and she were . . . well, she told me that you used to be together. But that must all be over now. Let's not . . ."

He frowned. "Oh, I have no intention of trying to rekindle anything—believe me. I just wondered if you knew."

"About you? Yes, I've just told you."

"No, not about me. About her."

I did not know what to say.

He lowered his voice. "You know that she's not who she says she is?"

"What?"

"She's not really called Jenny Parsons. And she's not a qualified teacher. Her name is something quite different—I never found it out—and she's . . . all right, I know you're not going to believe this, but I think she's wanted by the police."

I stared at him with utter incredulity. "The police? What are you talking about? Is this a joke?"

He shook his head. "Why should it be a joke? I don't know you, do I? I'm just warning you, pal. You're with some sort of confidence trickster. Not only that, but I think that she's . . ." He lowered his voice. "I think she's dangerous."

I wanted to burst out laughing. This was ridiculous. Here we were in broad daylight in a Paris hotel and a complete stranger was telling me that my girlfriend was dangerous. "Oh, come on . . ."

"No, you just listen to me. Jenny is not who she says she is." He paused. "And here's another thing. If you're wondering why I'm keeping away from her, it's because, well, if I didn't I think my life would be in danger."

There was something about his manner now that worried me. Although I might have written him off a few moments earlier as either a practical joker or a mental health case, it now crossed my mind that he was entirely serious. "Look," I said. "Tell me exactly why you think this. You can hardly expect . . ."

He cut me short. "Sorry," he said. "I can't say much more than that. Just think about what I've said, okay? Think about it."

His unsettling message delivered, with a final,

worried glance he slipped past me and continued downstairs. I stood where I was, unsure what to do. It was a good few minutes before I reminded myself that I was meant to be fetching the guide to Paris and that Jenny would be outside in the street waiting for me. If she really was Jenny, of course . . . I put the doubt out of my mind. Things like that did not happen; they simply did not. And yet, what if he were telling the truth? How well did I know Jenny? I asked myself. It was all very well to pick up somebody at a railway station, but what would one know about her? Everything that you knew would be learned from her, and how could I trust her? What if her whole story were untrue from start to finish? I remembered a friend saying to me once, "I can always tell whether somebody's lying to me. It's easy; you just **know** it." I had been doubtful. "I can't," I had said.

SHE NOTICED IMMEDIATELY THAT SOMEthing was wrong. She was looking in the window of a patisserie when I caught up with her.

"Mouth-watering," she said. "Look at that cake over there . . ." She broke off. "Was everything all right at the hotel?"

I avoided her gaze. "Yes. Fine."

I tried to keep my voice normal, but my distraction must have shown because she reached out and touched me on the forearm.

"Are you sure? You look as if you've seen something . . ."

"Something nasty in the woodshed," I joked. "Remember Aunt Ada Doom in **Cold Comfort Farm**? She saw something nasty in the woodshed and it affected her for life. Nobody ever found out what it was."

"I haven't read it. We had it at home, I seem to recall, but I haven't read it."

I found myself thinking: **What home? The home you told me about—the one in Durham—or is that entirely fictional?**

"It's very funny," I said, still trying to sound as normal as possible. But I was aware of the incongruity of the situation. We were looking in the window of a Parisian patisserie, admiring the cakes, and I was talking about English comic novels.

"Where's the guide?" she asked.

I felt in my pocket. I thought that I had put it there, but it was empty. I put my hand to my forehead in a gesture of confessed stupidity. "I must have left it in the room," I said.

"But you went there to fetch it."

"Yes, I know I did. But I must have been thinking of something else. You know how you can go somewhere to do something and then completely forget that you were meant to do it. You must have done that yourself."

She shook her head. "Look, Hugh, something

happened, didn't it?" She had fixed me with an intense stare, and I felt extremely uncomfortable. I averted my eyes. "No, don't look away. Don't deny it. Something happened . . . You saw Johnny. That's it. You saw him, didn't you?"

I nodded. "Yes. I met him on the stairs."

"And he said something? He did, didn't he?"

I was silent, trying to decide what to do.

"He told you something about me, didn't he? Go on: tell me. Tell me what he said."

I found it impossible to resist this examination. "Yes. He said something or other."

"Oh yes? What exactly?"

I almost told her, but then something stopped me; something made me afraid to do so. I looked away. "Nothing in particular."

She gripped my arm more tightly. "Come on, Hugh, I wasn't born yesterday. He said something. Of course you remember it. It's what's making you so peculiar right now. Tell me. You know it won't be true—you know that, don't you?"

"He said . . ."

She interrupted me to encourage me. "I can just imagine what he said. He said something about my not being a proper teacher? Is that what he said?"

I could see that she was angry—not with me, but with Johnny. "Something like that. It took me by surprise, and so I suppose I didn't take everything in."

She shook her head, as if to dispel her anger. "He's completely lost the place, you know. He's . . . deluded. It's bizarre."

Her denial, which gave every impression of sincerity, reassured me. "Yes, it was a bit like that."

She explained that he had not wanted to end their relationship and had tried everything to keep it going. "He was so possessive—ridiculously so. He wanted to know where I was all the time and whom I was seeing. He expected me to be at his beck and call, and if I was an hour or two late in returning his calls or text messages he'd become very suspicious. I couldn't cope with this. Who could?"

"I'm not surprised," I said. "It must have been suffocating."

"It was. And then when eventually I decided that I couldn't take it any longer and told him that we needed to break it off, he went ballistic. I thought that I'd have to tell the police about it, but then, the moment I threatened to do that, he backed off. But I know that he said some ridiculous things to some of my friends."

"Weird."

"Yes. Weird." She drew in her breath, as if girding herself for action. "I should do something about him."

I leaned forward and gave her a kiss. "Listen, this is a romantic break in Paris. I'm not going to allow some jealous creep to ruin it, are you?"

Her face broke into a smile. "No, I'm not."

"And we don't really need the guidebook," I said. "We can get by perfectly well without it."

"Of course we can. We can go where the spirit moves us."

We wandered off. We had lunch in a restaurant on the Île de la Cité and then walked along the banks of the river, looking at the stalls selling prints and books. Then we went to the Louvre, which she had never visited before. I showed her my favourite picture—Ghirlandaio's picture of the old man with the bulbous nose returning his grandson's look of wonderment. She liked the Vuillards best: "So comfortable," she said. "People doing ordinary things—ironing, arranging flowers and so on. I love them."

The day went past very quickly. At six o'clock we returned to the hotel, had showers and changed. Then we went out for dinner again, and it was there that I told her that as far as I was concerned this was the most wonderful love affair I had ever had. She said that she felt the same.

"I'm so lucky that I found you on that railway platform," I said. "And you weren't even in a handbag."

She looked puzzled. "Oscar Wilde," I said. "**The Importance of Being Earnest.** One of the characters was found as a baby in a handbag on a railway station. So Lady Bracknell says, 'A handbag?' It's one of the best-known lines in drama."

She laughed. "And would it have made any difference if I had been in a handbag?"

"None at all," I said.

After that, we sat for a few moments in complete silence. She was looking at the menu, and I let my gaze wander to a neighbouring table. An imposing-looking woman was seated opposite a neat, rather fussy man, considerably smaller than she was. He was wearing a yellow waistcoat, his dash of colour, I thought—his statement. They were a very conventional couple, I decided; safe in every respect . . . Safe. I looked back at Jenny, and caught her eye. She smiled at me, but I noticed a slight hesitation before the smile, as if she was unsure what I was thinking and how she should react. It occurred to me that everything she had said about Johnny might be untrue, and that her hesitation sprang from her uncertainty as to whether she had been believed. She was judging me, perhaps, determining the degree of my gullibility. I looked away. No. No. I believed her; of course I believed her. How could you not believe somebody with whom you had travelled to Paris and with whom you were having dinner and telling just how much you liked her?

NO, THOUGHT ANDREW. NO. YOU DIDN'T really know her. It was just sex. Be honest. It was different with us—I would still want to be with Hermione even if sex had never been invented. Would I? Yes, I would. Definitely. But that was not what he was going to speak about. He was going to say something more about Hermione's father.

"HE CLAIMED TO BE FOND OF HER," HE SAID. "But would any parent who loved his daughter—and I mean really loved his daughter—have done what he did? At the time, I didn't think so. I thought in his case it was more a matter of ego. Hermione was one of his possessions, so to speak. He thought he owned her, in that same way that he owned his business. She was an adornment, and he wasn't having just anybody taking her away from him. The person who did that had to match up to him as well as to Hermione."

Kay nodded. "Sounds familiar. Possessiveness. Ambition. There are plenty of people like that about. And it can be difficult, you know, for a parent to accept that a son or daughter is being taken away from them by somebody else. You have to see it from their point of view—particularly where it's a case of father and daughter or mother and son."

"Are those worse?"

"They tend to be. Mothers can be more possessive of sons than they are of daughters, and the same with fathers and daughters—at least in my experience. But did he ruin it for you?"

"He tried to."

"How?"

I DON'T THINK HE SAID ANYTHING TO HER, or at least he didn't say anything specific. That would have been a bit too heavy-handed: **You're not to see that young man any more!** Nobody in his right mind says anything that direct any more, I would have thought. That would be an invitation for anybody to tell the parent to get lost. Obviously.

No, he was more subtle than that, I think. She talked to me about it and told me how he did it. He invited her to various things, but just her, and never me. She went out of loyalty, and then discovered that there were all sorts of young men invited as well—by her father. Surprise, surprise! And these young men, it turned out, were all very attentive to her, having been encouraged by her father. I said that was subtle, and it doesn't sound much like it—but it was difficult for her to prove anything. It was just a clear indication that he was keen for her to find an alternative to me. Of course, he might not have achieved what he wanted. If she had fallen for any of these rivals, then he might have had to do something about that as well.

He tried to fill her time so as to squeeze me out. He suggested that she should accompany him to Paris, to St. Petersburg, to all sorts of places. Of course she was meant to be working in the auction house while all this was going on, and so she had an excuse not to go. But do you know what he did? He went and spoke to his friend, the chairman, and fixed it that she could take time off. She was furious, but somehow she found it impossible to stand up to him. I suppose he was just too strong a personality, and when you have a father like that, there's not much you can do, other than walk away.

I said to her once, "Hermione, sooner or later you're going to have to choose. Do you let your father run your life, or do you make your own decisions? It's that simple."

The question upset her. She said that she loved him for all his faults. "And what's wrong with loving your father?" she asked.

"Nothing. But you can't let him dictate your life for you. You have to have . . . your own emotional space."

"Emotional space! You're sounding like . . ."

"A problem page. Okay, I admit it. But it's true, isn't it? And the idea of emotional space sums it up, if you ask me."

"Well, I need emotional space to think about this. So please don't pressurise me."

"Pressurise you? Now you're sounding like . . . like the instruction manual for an inflatable mattress."

"So that's what I am to you? An inflatable mattress?"

"I never said that. Don't be ridiculous."

You can see that it did not exactly help our relationship.

THEN HE HAD THE MOST SPECTACULAR FALL. It happens, you know: one moment somebody is at the top of his game. Everything is going his way. He has power, influence, the admiration of the public. And then he does something that brings the whole edifice down about his ears.

There are plenty of examples, and we all know about them: politicians who are discovered to have been fiddling their expenses; government ministers who have been getting too cosy with crooked businessmen; judges with gambling debts or secret mistresses. There are so many ways of falling off the high moral ground you've carefully built up for yourself. Moral ground is like that—slippery at the edges.

27

THE FIRST THING I KNEW OF IT WAS FROM the newspapers. It was on page one. Hermione's father had been accused of insider trading. I've never understood exactly what's involved in that, but apparently this was a bad case of it and the papers said that the City of London was shocked. I gather it's a tight community and if you tread on toes they certainly let you know all about it. But in his case there was more to it than that. The investigations into the insider trading had also revealed that he had abused his position as trustee for a very large and very popular charity. According to the reports I read, he had enriched himself at the expense of the charity. It was complicated, but it seems that the charity needed a certain consultation job done. Hermione's father had fixed things so that this contract was given to a company that he himself controlled. The company was not the lowest bidder for the work; in fact, it was the highest.

Now this charity was concerned with the welfare of the children of servicemen who had been killed or wounded in action. It's difficult to imagine a more sensitive cause, and the idea of defrauding something like that was about as distasteful as one can imagine. People were outraged, and had there been a mob, it would have strung him up on a lamppost.

So from being an eminently respectable and highly influential citizen, Hermione's father had suddenly become a pariah.

"DROPPED BY HIS FRIENDS, I SUPPOSE," said Kay.

Andrew nodded. "Yes. Hermione told me later that he saw people cross the street if they saw him coming. To the other side, of course."

"Then they weren't friends," said Hugh.

David agreed with this. "Can't have been. Real friends stick with you."

"Even if you do something really shocking? I mean, really shocking?" Kay asked.

David thought for a moment. "I think so. People convicted of serial killing get visitors in prison, don't they?"

"From people as depraved as they are," suggested Andrew.

David was not sure. They might be, he said. Or they might just be people who recognised that there was still a person there who was worthy of their friendship. And people forgave people, he said. They did. They forgave.

Kay smiled. "Just as well, because . . ."

They looked at her, waiting. "Because what?" asked Hugh.

"Ever been forgiven?" she said.

FORGIVENESS, THOUGHT ANDREW, AND THEN continued: Hermione stayed away from work on the day that the news broke. I telephoned her at her flat and on her mobile, but she did not answer. I left a message, asking her to call me back. She did that eventually, just before ten that evening. I told her that I could understand why she would not want to speak to anybody, but I thought it would help if we could meet.

"It won't," she said tearfully. "Nothing will help now. I can't face anything or anybody. I just can't."

I tried to persuade her to let me see her, but she would not even tell me where she was. She was not in London, she said, and there was no point in my trying to look for her. She would phone me in a few days' time, she hoped, but she could not be sure.

There was more about the scandal in the paper the following day. Her father's enemies—of whom there was a very large number—had a field-day. He had been convicted of nothing, the papers were at pains to point out, but that did not stop people recounting incidents of his arrogant behaviour. Nobody, it seemed, had a good word to say about him.

Hermione came back to work the day after that. I wanted to talk about what had happened, as I was keen to tell her that as far as I was concerned what her father had or had not done was nothing to do with her, and certainly nothing to do with my feelings for her. She heard me out, her head sunk in her hands, avoiding looking at me.

I think it helped. At the end, she allowed me to take her hand and to hold it.

"You've been kind," she said. "Unlike everybody else. But let's leave it at that. I can't bear to talk about it any more."

"Is he all right?" I asked.

"He's gone silent," she said. "He barely says a word. And his eyes are glazed, as if he's concussed." She lowered her voice. "I think he'll probably kill himself."

I sought to reassure her. "I don't think so. He must be tougher than that."

"No, he's not. The toughness is all a façade. He's actually very vulnerable."

"Well, maybe this will change him. Have you thought of that? Have you thought that he might become a different person after this?"

She shook her head. "I don't think so. I think he's just going to give up, that's all."

I said nothing after that. I had no real sympathy for her father; after all, he had been caught out engaged in despicable activities; what was there to sympathise with? And if he was going to be punished, then it was well-deserved and would probably involve less suffering than he had caused for others in his long and ruthless business career. No, I decided, I would certainly not shed any tears for a man like that.

HERMIONE AND I CONTINUED TO SEE EACH other over the weeks that followed, but she seemed distracted—understandably, in the circumstances—and the passion was cooling. I came to the conclusion that even if we continued with our affair for the rest of the summer, it would not last beyond that. I felt disappointed; I had cherished great hopes for it.

Then, three weeks after the first disclosures had been made public, I saw him in one of those streets that run west off Regent Street. It was during my lunch hour, and I had decided to make a quick visit to an exhibition that was on at the Royal Academy in Piccadilly. I knew that the exhibition would be more crowded at lunchtime, but it only had a few days left to run and I did not want to miss it.

As I turned a corner, I found myself in front of a shoe shop. Something caught my eye in the window—a pair of monk shoes—and I stopped to look. The shoes were vastly too expensive for me on my student budget, but I could still see myself in them. I studied the shoes, which were brown, buffed to a high gloss. They were beautiful. Then I noticed him through the glass sitting in the shop, a few shoe boxes in front of him. As I noticed him, he looked up and our eyes met.

My first reaction was to turn my head away and pretend that I had not seen him. But I could not do this. I nodded, and he acknowledged this with a nod of his own head. Then he stood up, said something to the assistant who had returned with a further box of shoes, and came out to speak to me.

"Oh," I said. "I was just looking at some shoes and I saw you . . ."

"Yes. I saw that."

"You've found what you were looking for?" It was a trite thing to say, but he seemed not to mind.

"Later. I'll find something later. I go through shoes rather quickly for some reason. I think I must be hard on them." He glanced at his watch. "I wanted to thank you by the way. My daughter says that you've been very supportive. Thank you for that."

I nodded. "She's been upset."

He nodded.

Then, without having thought about it, I said, "And I was very sorry to hear that things have been so hard for you. People like kicking people when they're down, don't they?"

He was surprised by my comment. "You don't think I deserve it?"

I shrugged. "I don't know. I don't know exactly what you're meant to have done. You haven't been convicted of anything, have you?"

He was staring at me. "I've been informed that the insider trading charges will not be pursued after all. And as for the matter of the improper allocation of the charity's contract, what if I were to tell you that I had no knowledge of it, that it was arranged by my assistant, who did not see fit to tell me about it."

I looked into his eyes. "If you said that . . ."

"Yes, I am saying that."

"Then I would give you the benefit of the doubt."

"You would?"

"Yes. I think I believe you."

Our eyes were still locked. "So you don't think that I'm getting what I deserved? Isn't that what everybody says?"

"No." I took a deep breath. He had asked me a question and I should answer it truthfully. "Some people probably think that. Maybe quite a few."

He began to smile. "You're very direct."

"Where I come from, people are direct. It's like that in Scotland. You speak your mind."

His smile broadened. "So I see." He hesitated before continuing. "I was rude to you, I think. I wrote you off as somebody for Hermione."

"I could tell that."

"And I was wrong. I want you to accept my apology."

I think my surprise showed.

"I mean it," he said. "I want to say sorry."

"Thank you."

"And as for Hermione . . ."

I stopped him. "I think that it's cooling off. On her side, anyway . . ."

He frowned. "I'm sorry to hear that. I'd be very happy if it continued."

I smiled. "So would I. I really like her . . ."

"I can tell that."

There was a moment of silence. I felt awkward, and wondered how long this encounter would last. He showed no signs of wanting to bring it to an end.

"I think that she might be pleased to hear that I approved of you."

I hesitated. I did not want him to interfere—and neither, I imagined, did Hermione. "I'm not sure . . ."

"Not that I'm going to get involved. It's her affair."

"Yes."

He offered his hand for me to shake. I took it.

"Now I'd better go back in there and get those shoes."

"Yes."

He seemed suddenly to think of something. "Which shoes were you looking at?"

I pointed at the monk shoes in the display. "I've always liked that style."

He took hold of my arm and led me towards the door of the shop. "They're yours. On me."

"I can't . . ."

"Of course you can."

28

KAY CLAPPED HER HANDS TOGETHER. "OH, very nice! Very nice! A happy ending. Or at least, I assume it was a happy ending . . ."

"It was. Hermione and I are still together. Everything's going well. I'm going to marry her eventually—I just know it."

"But does she? Does she know it?"

"I think she suspects it."

"And what about her father? What became of him?"

"She said he changed a bit. Not altogether, but she said that she thought he was different. He had had a shock, I think, to discover that so many people hated him. That had some effect."

"It sometimes does." She looked at me enquiringly. "And now?"

"I've graduated."

"Congratulations."

"Thank you."

"And what next?"

"They gave me a job at the auction house. A real job. That's what I'm going to."

"You must be very pleased. You said that it was very competitive."

"It is. But Eleanor backed me. She said that that business with the train swung it."

"Ah! So missing a train can have major consequences."

"You could say that."

29

NEAT, THOUGHT DAVID. A NEAT ENDING. IN love. Out of love. A new job. Begin again. Find somebody else. But it's not always that easy to find somebody else, and you may not want to because the person you found earlier was the person you wanted to be with. And so what did you do? You got on with your life and tried not to think too much about it. And you could develop a particular trick—a trick that he had never discussed with anybody else but which worked. You took pleasure in the happiness of others. It was that simple. You may not have had what you want in life, but many did, and that was something to bear in mind. So I'm glad for you, Andrew, that you had that summer and that it was so good for you and that you got the job you wanted.

But he remembered this: the following summer, making the trip to Maine and finding that his boat, upturned in a neighbour's boathouse to keep it safe over the winter, was covered inside with cobwebs. He had cleared these out with an old broom, bringing to an end the intricate cities that spiders had spun for themselves. And then, with the boat launched, he had allowed the current to take him, rocking the boat and twisting it in its eddies, until he was level with the point where he drew close with the house belonging to Bruce's family. From the river there was a view of the yard at the back, and the tree under which the professor of mathematics parked his grey car. There was no sign of life; they came irregularly, Bruce had said; his father was given to acting on whim, and might just as easily suggest that the summer be spent in somewhere unpromising—they had holidayed one year in Pittsburgh, which was hardly getting away at all, but which had coincided with an opportunity he had been given to teach a summer school there.

The next day, he did the same, with the same result. The house and its yard had a slightly dishevelled look to it, as some of the summer houses did. It could have done with a lick of paint; it could have done with somebody cutting back the blackcurrant bushes that were taking over and obscuring the fence; presumably the professor of mathematics was above all that.

Then, the following week, when he had concluded that Bruce was spending the summer somewhere else, he saw the grey car under the tree and noticed that the door of the back porch was open. He stopped rowing, and let the boat drift. His heart was pounding as he slipped the oars back into the rowlocks and began to row himself home. He would give it an hour or two—they might just have arrived—and then he could ride past the house and drop in because he had seen the car. He did not want Bruce to think that he had been watching.

But Bruce revealed that he, too, had been anxious. "I was hoping you'd be here," he said. "I wanted to do some fishing. I thought maybe you'd been and gone again."

The words thrilled him. **I was hoping you'd be here.**

There followed ten days in which they shared their boats, fished, or went for burgers at the diner. Bruce seemed to enjoy his company, but there remained at the back of David's mind the fear that this friendship meant far more to him than it did to Bruce. Bruce spoke of other high school friends and of a girl in Princeton whose mother worked in his father's department and of whom he wanted to see rather more. They planned to go to New York some day to see some people she knew.

"You could come to my place in New York," said David. "Any time. Bring her." He hoped that Bruce would come by himself, but he said this out of politeness.

"Maybe," said Bruce. "We'll see. She's got her own ideas. She's full of them."

"Such as?"

Bruce shrugged. "You know how girls are. They think differently." He paused, and looked at David. "You must know some girls round here . . . How about we go and see them? How about that?"

David looked away. "I don't really know any. Maybe one or two, but not very well."

The subject of the visit to New York was dropped. David thought: It's another year before I'll see him again after this. Another year, and then he'll be here again for only a week or two and it'll be another year after that.

He came to him in his dreams. He was by the river somewhere, at a spot where there were trees and a high bank, and Bruce was standing with him on the bank. Bruce was looking at him and smiling, and then he took a step forward and put his arms about him and said, **You're the best friend I've ever had, David, you know that?** And he felt that there was so much that he wanted to say, but could neither speak nor move. And then Bruce somehow was not there; he just was no longer there, but for a few moments, more precious than any others, he had felt complete union with the boy whom he loved so much that it ached. When he awoke, he felt as if he had been vouchsafed a vision, and the night about him, and all the world beyond the night, was golden and glowing.

They were together for ten days the following year, and for just under two weeks the year after that. They spoke of college plans. Bruce was applying to Oberlin; he had an uncle who had been there and the uncle, who had a successful engineering business, had offered to pay his tuition.

"And you, David? What about you?"

"I'm going to try for Princeton."

"Princeton! My hometown. That'll be great."

"Maybe we'll see one another around."

Bruce was uncertain. "Probably not. I'll be at Oberlin when you're in Princeton, and in the summer when I'm in Princeton you're usually here."

"I'll get a job. Maybe I can stay in Princeton over the summer if I'm working."

Bruce was doubtful. "It's not a big place. There aren't many jobs. There are some coffee bars and so on, I suppose. You could cut grass, that sort of thing, I guess, but it's not like New York, you know. You'd earn much more in New York." He smiled and punched his friend playfully on the upper arm. "Princeton. Just think of that."

30

THEY DID SEE ONE ANOTHER IN PRINCETON in spite of Bruce's predictions. David made a point of going to college early, several weeks before the academic year began. Bruce had not yet set off for Oberlin and David called him at home shortly after he had arrived. They met in a coffee bar near the university bookstore; David was laden with books from his advance reading list.

"Philosophy," said Bruce, picking one of the books out of the bookstore bag. "Is that going to be your major?"

"Yes. I thought of English, but I decided this was more interesting."

Bruce read the title of the book he had picked out. "**The Examined Life**. What's this about?"

"It's about how we should live our lives, I think. I haven't read it yet. I flicked through it in the bookstore. I think it's really interesting."

Bruce opened a page at random and read a few sentences. "Yes. Maybe."

"Somebody said that the unexamined life was not worth leading. I forget who. But I heard that once."

"So you should know what you're doing? Is that it?"

David considered this. "I think it's more than that. Sure, you have to know what you're doing, but I think it's more about looking at the things you do and asking yourself **why** you do them."

"That's what psychology is all about, isn't it? Is philosophy the same thing as psychology?"

"No. Psychology comes into it, but I think it's more about making sense of your life. The bit that I read was going on about how many people lead their lives without ever having any real plan—any pattern. They just do stuff without thinking how it fits with the things they did before or the things they want to do in the future."

"So that's what life should be like? Knowing what you want? Is that it?"

"Yes."

Bruce flicked a few pages. "He says here that people should look at their friendships and ask themselves what the friendships mean to them." He looked up from the book. "But our friends are just . . . just the people we get on with. That's all."

David reached for the book. "Let me see."

He looked at the page. **Our friendships reveal the contours of the self, what we really are; or at least the examined friendship is capable of doing that.** He read a few more sentences and then closed the book.

He looked at Bruce, who was smiling back at him. He wanted to lean forward and embrace him. He wanted to weep. He wanted to say: **Can't you see**

what I'm feeling? Can't you? But of course he could not do that. He could never do that. It was not permitted. It was not possible. But most of all, he sensed that what he felt simply was not reciprocated. Bruce did not love him as he loved Bruce. That was the way of it. Oil and water. Salt water and fresh. Different.

Bruce came back home on a few occasions that first year, and always called David when he did so. They met up, and Bruce took him to parties; he knew a lot of people in Princeton and David acquired some of these friends too. They went to New York together, more than once, and stayed with David's parents. In the summer of their second year at college, they travelled to Ireland and Scotland together. Bruce's father was of Scottish extraction—three generations back—and his mother was Boston Irish. He wanted company on the trip that his grandparents were funding, and he invited David.

They spent three days in Dublin and a couple of days in Kerry. In Kerry they stayed in Dingle, a fishing town, and drank too much Guinness one night in a pub in which they had been listening to some folk singers and a traditional fiddler. They made their way back to the hostel they were staying in, full of music and dark ale.

"I love this country, you know," said Bruce. "I don't want to go back home. Ever."

"Me too," said David. "I don't want to leave. I want to stay. We could both stay. We could buy . . .

buy a farm and live there and raise pigs or whatever. Brew Guinness maybe."

"And each marry one of those Irish girls with clear skin and dark hair," said Bruce.

David said nothing.

Bruce stopped. "If that's what you wanted to do," he muttered. "You don't have to, you know."

David looked away. "Marry an Irish girl? I don't know."

"It's not for everybody," said Bruce. And then he said, affecting an Irish accent. "Look at the moon up there, would you? What's that line in the play you were telling me about—**Juno and . . .**"

"**Juno and the Paycock**. Sean O'Casey. It's: **What is the moon, Captain? That's the question. What is the moon?** It's said by a character called Joxer Daly."

Bruce burst out laughing. "What is the moon, David? That's the question. What is the moon?"

David looked up at the sky. Above the outline of roofs with chimneys, a church spire, the moon hung over Ireland, an almost full moon, benign, it seemed to him, tolerant of so much . . .

"The moon is all about love," he said. "The moon is about how we love others. About how we just want the best for those we love. We want them to be happy. We want everything to work out for them. The moon wants that for us, you know. That's what the moon is."

"The moon!" exclaimed Bruce. "That's lovely, David. That's lovely poetry. And you made it up right here, just because I asked some stupid question about what the moon was. You knew all along! You knew what the moon was about!"

"I made it up for you," muttered David. He spoke quietly, half hoping that his friend would not hear.

But he did. "That's what I said. You made it up for me."

WHEN THEY REACHED SCOTLAND, THEY made for Skye and the islands of the Outer Hebrides. They hitched a lift to South Uist and stayed in a farmhouse that offered accommodation. They stayed six days, taking up most of the time they had allocated for their Scottish journey. But neither wanted to move, just as they had felt that they wanted to stay in Ireland forever. The island was part of a small archipelago that was the last bastion of Scotland against the cold green waves of the Atlantic. They walked its length and breadth. Their host showed them the **machair,** the strip of land that separated the beach from the pasture behind: a delicate ribbon of grass and flowers, resistant to the salt that sprayed across it, its soil whitened by tiny fragments of shells.

"Machair," said Bruce, savouring the word. "Machair. You know, if I ever have a daughter, I'll call her Machair. How about that?"

"A good name," agreed David.

It was midsummer, and the nights of the north of Scotland did not get dark until just before midnight, and then, a few hours later, lightened again. They went fishing on a loch with rods borrowed from their host.

"You boys have fitted in pretty well," said the farmer.

"Scottish blood," said Bruce. "It tells, doesn't it?"

"You must come back some day. You're always welcome."

AT THE END OF THEIR TRIP, WHEN THEY landed at JFK, they went their separate ways. They stood for a few moments outside the terminal, their backpacks at their feet. They were tired from the journey.

"Well, I guess it's goodbye," said Bruce.

David looked down at his hands. They had caught the sun, and the wind, in the Hebrides. They were like the hands of one of those fishermen, he suddenly thought. "Yes. Thanks for everything."

Bruce stepped forward and put a hand on his shoulder. "Yes. Thank you, too, for coming with me. And . . ."

David looked up, and met his friend's gaze. **You don't have to say it**, he thought.

"And I want you to know that it meant a lot to me—that trip, having you there as a friend. That night in Dingle . . ."

"**What is the moon, Captain?** " said David, smiling. I can smile through this, he thought. I can still smile through it.

"Yes, what is the moon, Captain? You gave the answer, didn't you?"

"Maybe. I don't know. I don't really remember."

"Well you did. And I remember it."

"Well then, I did."

31

THAT WAS TWENTY-FIVE YEARS AGO. DURING that time, they saw one another occasionally, but not very often. Sometimes a year or two would pass between meetings, which were usually in New York, when Bruce was passing through the city for some reason. He lived in Washington, where he worked for an organisation that promoted conservation. He had specialised in environmental science and was full of worrying statistics on the consequences of pollution and deforestation. He had married a biologist who worked for the federal government. They had two children. Both were boys, and so there was no opportunity to use the name Machair, which he had never forgotten.

David eventually left New York and took a job at a college in Buffalo. He kept the family apartment in New York, though, and was often down in the city. His father had left him a surprisingly large inheritance that he could have lived on if he had wished. But he enjoyed teaching philosophy and ran a popular course entitled "The Examined Life."

"Don't expect me to teach you how to live your lives," he said to his students at the beginning of each year. "I can't provide you with the answers to that. But I can teach you how to ask questions, even if these questions may strike you as unanswerable." Such as: **What is the moon?** he thought.

David married too. She taught English at the same college. He was a kind and considerate husband, and he loved his wife, and she loved him. There was nothing wrong with the marriage; nothing. They had a daughter whom he could not call Machair. That was Bruce's name for the daughter he had never had, and it would have been an act of expropriation.

"Your friend, Bruce," she said. "We should get them up here some time."

"Maybe," he said.

Nobody knew about what he felt; and why should they be told? There is no reason why we should not have our secrets, as long as those secrets do not harm anybody else. His harmed nobody, although sometimes he thought that it would help him if he were able to tell somebody about it. Perhaps it would bring him some sort of catharsis; perhaps it would not. It was safer, he thought, to keep it to himself; because there are many ways of loving, and anyway, nothing had ever happened between the two of them; it had been innocent, unsullied. Everything is possible in love. In the heart of each of us there can be many rooms, and sometimes there are.

"BY THE TIME WE LEFT PARIS," SAID HUGH, "I had more or less forgotten about Johnny Bates. I knew that there were some people who couldn't let go when a relationship came to an end, and I assumed that he was just one of those. I knew that some of these people could grow into full-blown stalkers, but it seemed to me that he was confining himself to spreading ridiculous rumours about Jenny. That was bad enough, but at least he wasn't actively pursuing her, which would have been much more worrying for her."

WITH THE EXCEPTION OF THAT INCIDENT with Johnny, the Paris trip had gone well. I know that the romantic Parisian get-away can be a bit of a cliché, but it worked for both of us. I got to know Jenny much better, and appreciated her qualities. She was fun to be with. She was amusing. She took pleasure in small, ridiculous things, just as I did. For example, when we saw a fussily clipped white poodle being taken for a walk along a boulevard by its owner, a woman dressed up to the nines, neither of us could keep a straight face. Then we witnessed a wonderful, sparky Gallic row involving a taxi driver and a pedestrian, which drew an appreciative and demonstrative crowd. We saw a vain policeman admiring and adjusting his uniform in the reflective window of a glove shop. We saw children carrying baguettes back home. All of these were small things, but somehow it seemed wonderful to be experiencing them in Paris and to be able to share them with somebody who looked on the world in the same way. I had the occasional doubt—yes—but they were just passing thoughts, really, and I made an effort to dismiss them. It is not always easy to put things out of your mind, but I succeeded—for the most part. It just seemed so implausible; possible—just—but pretty unlikely.

You might have imagined that the magic stopped at the airport, and to a great extent it did. When we arrived back in London, the skies were overcast and heavy. The bus driver from the airport was morose and unkempt; the streets seemed run-down and dirty, the people sour-faced. But that, I suspect, is how coming home is for everyone; Parisians probably felt the same when they returned from elsewhere.

I returned to Edinburgh, and Jenny caught a train back to the West Country. She saw me off at Kings Cross station before she went off to Paddington. We kissed at the ticket barrier, interrupting the flow of people onto the platform.

"Perform fond farewells elsewhere, if you don't mind," said the man at the barrier.

"That wouldn't have happened in Paris," muttered Jenny.

Back in Edinburgh, I telephoned her every evening, as we planned our next meeting. I was determined now to get to London, and to get her there, too, if I could manage it. In pursuit of this, I applied to the company for a temporary transfer that had been advertised internally. One of the company's London employees was going to be away for a year doing an MBA, and the post needed to be filled. I think that I must have fitted the requirements exactly, as the personnel department telephoned me immediately and said that if I wanted the posting it was mine. I accepted.

"Now we can see one another every weekend," I said to Jenny. "Maybe even more often."

She said she was pleased. She had been thinking of applying for a job herself in London, but felt that we should wait and see how the new arrangement worked out. She enjoyed her job in Gloucestershire, and would prefer it, she felt, to teaching in London, which was more stressful. I agreed.

So I left Edinburgh and moved to a flat in Notting Hill. It was a more expensive flat than I could ever have afforded myself, but it belonged to a friend who had taken a job in the City and had done well. He had a spare room that he was keen to let out, and we knew that we got on well enough to share. It was the perfect solution from my point of view as Colin, my friend, spent most weekends with his girlfriend in Canterbury, and that would mean that Jenny and I would have the flat to ourselves.

Our lives settled into a pattern. She arrived in London at five on Friday afternoons. That evening we would go out to dinner, and then on Saturday we would enjoy what London had to offer, going to exhibitions, to the cinema or theatre, browsing in Portobello Market, which was just a few blocks away from where I lived. We built up a new circle of friends, too, and would have these friends round to dinner on Saturday night, or go out with them to a gastro-pub or Indian restaurant. Life was very enjoyable, and I was already trying to work out a means of prolonging the year, even if it meant switching to a new company.

From time to time, rather than Jenny coming to London, I would go to stay with her. This was generally more difficult, as the house she shared with the other two teachers was minuscule, and there was barely room for a fourth person. But it was a change from our London routine, and we both enjoyed it. Shopping and theatre were replaced by country walks and the occasional meal at The Lamb and Flag, where it all began.

It was on one of these weekends in Gloucestershire that I made my discovery. Jenny had gone out to buy something that she needed for the meal she was making and had left me in the house, reading the newspaper. I decided to tackle the crossword, which I occasionally do, although not very successfully. I needed a pencil to do this, and I thought I had seen one on the small writing desk that Jenny had in her room. I crossed the room to this desk.

The top drawer had been left open. This contained envelopes, a box of paper clips, and a bottle of correcting fluid of the sort that people used before the invention of printers. I picked up the bottle—it was an ancient relic, encrusted round the top with the white powder of its dried contents. I put it back. I found the pencil I was looking for, but then I noticed something that was half hidden by an envelope. It was a passport that had been cancelled and had the top right hand corner of its cover clipped off to signify the cancellation.

I picked it up and looked at it. The front pages bore a number of border stamps, and there was also an Indian visa. I turned to the back, where the personal details of the holder are set out. The passport belonged, it seemed, to one Mary Broughton. The photograph had been cut out of the page.

I was about to replace it, thinking that it must have belonged to some friend of Jenny's, when I happened to turn to the page that gave the details of relatives who might be contacted in the event of accident. This part is filled in by the passport-holder and in this case it gave two names, with addresses and phone numbers. One of these was of somebody who lived in Leeds, another was . . . I stopped. Johnny Bates, with an address in London.

Then I noticed something else. These names were written in handwriting that clearly belonged to Jenny.

Fumbling from the shock, I picked up the pencil and wrote down Johnny Bates' address and phone numbers on a piece of paper. Then I replaced the passport, slipped the piece of paper into my pocket, and closed the drawer. Returning to the crossword, I tried to apply my mind to it, but could not. What I had seen had shocked me so much that I could not concentrate. So I got up and returned to the desk to take another look at the passport.

"What are you doing?"

I spun round. Jenny had come back from the shops and was standing in the doorway of her room, carrying a large plastic bag. At moments of crisis, one notices odd little details, and I noticed that peeping out of the bulging shopping bag was a bulb of fennel.

"Fennel," I said. "I love fennel."

"But what are you doing?" repeated Jenny.

Fortunately I did not have the passport in my hands . . .

"A pencil," I said. "I was looking for a pencil." And then, in an innocent tone, "Are we having fennel tonight?"

She put the bag down, glancing at the desk as she did so. I moved away. "I'm not going to bother," I said. "I was going to do the crossword, but now that you're back I don't think I will."

"Suit yourself," she said. "I'm going to take this stuff to the kitchen."

I did not make the mistake of returning to the drawer once she had left the room, and just as well, for she came back a few seconds later. It struck me that she was testing me, that she had returned to see what I was doing, but I cannot be sure of that.

For the rest of that weekend I tried to put the incident out of my mind. When I did think of it, I said to myself that it was absurd to think that the passport told a sinister story. And yet there was the evidence of her handwriting, as well as the name of Johnny Bates. That pointed, surely, to the fact that Johnny had been right—that Jenny was really Mary Broughton.

I told myself that there must be an innocent explanation, even if I could not readily think of one. I reminded myself, too, that I had noticed Jenny's own name, written in her handwriting, in some of the books she kept in her room. She **was** Jenny—she had to be. No school employed anybody without proper checks on their qualifications and identity—had she been hiding anything, then surely the school authorities would have discovered it. Unless . . . unless she had assumed the identity of somebody else altogether, had stolen it. Such things happened. We were always being warned about identity theft, and although those warnings were mostly about credit cards, there were surely other, more dramatic, instances in which one person claimed to be another.

I tried to act normally, but I found it hard, and I think she noticed that there was something wrong.

"Are you feeling all right?" she asked. "You seem to be distracted."

I shrugged. "I'm feeling a bit out of sorts. I think that it might be some sort of mild bug I've picked up in London. Travelling in the Tube you get everything, I imagine."

She offered me a couple of aspirin, which I took. She watched me as I swallowed the pills, and it crossed my mind that she was watching to make sure that I actually took them and that I had not been bluffing. And then, no sooner had I swallowed them, the thought occurred to me: What if they weren't aspirin?

I went into the bathroom and locked the door behind me. Putting my finger down my throat, I tried to make myself sick. I retched—not too loudly I hoped—but the pills remained down. Then I saw on the basin a small bottle of pills. The label clearly said aspirin, and so I calmed down. "Don't be ridiculous," I said to myself. "Don't become like Johnny Bates—paranoid."

I returned to London a little earlier than I had originally planned. I had a genuine excuse for this—I had some work to finish before my first meeting at work the next morning, and Jenny said that she understood. At the same time, when we said goodbye, I think she sensed that something was wrong.

"I think you're feeling a bit down," she said. "Maybe it's a result of some virus you picked up. They can leave you feeling a bit weak, a bit depressed, I think."

"Yes," I said. "That's probably it."

33

IN LONDON I TOOK OUT THE SLIP OF PAPER on which I had written Johnny Bates' contact address and phone numbers. I dialled his mobile first, but it quickly switched to answering mode. I left a brief message, asking him to phone me, and then I tried the other number on the card, a land-line.

The phone rang at the other end but was soon answered. A man's voice answered: a Liverpool accent. It was not Johnny. I assumed it was a flat-mate, perhaps one of the other two men we had seen him with in Paris.

"I'd like to speak to Johnny," I said. "Johnny Bates."

"So would I," said the voice.

"I'm sorry?"

"I'd like to speak to him too. Johnny's gone off somewhere without telling us."

For a few moments I said nothing.

The nasal voice sounded irritated. "Are you still there?"

"Sorry. Yes, I'm still here. Is Johnny all right?"

"How do we know?" said the voice, peevishly. "We're on the point of reporting him missing. If he's not back by tomorrow morning we're going to do that."

"What about home? Has he got family anywhere?"

"We've spoken to them. They're in the dark too."

I asked whether he had done this before. Perhaps it was his job. Perhaps he was working somewhere else for a few weeks.

A snort of derision came down the line. "Job? You obviously don't know Johnny very well. Ever seen Johnny do any work? I haven't."

I concluded the call and sat back in my chair. What had Jenny said? **I should do something about him**. It was an appalling thought. No, it was impossible. And yet Johnny had said, very deliberately and as if he really meant it: **I think my life would be in danger.**

I closed my eyes. These things did not happen in real life—in fiction, yes, because you suspend disbelief in novels, but not in the everyday world about us. You simply don't meet women on the run from the police at railway stations. And these women don't then make muttered threats against men who have tumbled to their secret, and then carry these threats out. It doesn't happen.

IT WAS JENNY'S TURN TO COME TO LONDON the following weekend. I toyed with the idea of calling the visit off, but when she telephoned me a day or two later everything sounded so normal and she seemed to be so looking forward to the trip that I said nothing.

"I can't wait to come," she said. "It's turning into a dreadful week at school. The kids are all excited about their sports day and being hyper in the classroom. I've had three pant-wettings, two full-scale punch ups, and one case of aggravated hair-pulling—and that's by Wednesday."

I had to laugh. "Occupational hazards."

"Yes. Remember those films where the children sat at desks all in a row, even the small kids. They sat at their desks and weren't allowed to get up without permission. What happened?"

"The nineteen-sixties."

"Yes?"

"That's when it started."

"But conditions were dreadful before that," she said. "Somebody like Mary Lewis would have been slapped for her pains."

"Mary Lewis?"

She explained that Mary Lewis was the girl who stood accused of pulling another girl's pigtails. "She comes from a badly behaved family," she went on. "Her brother set fire to a farmer's barn, and the father, I gather, is a well-known thief."

I listened to this and then, without really thinking about it, I said, "Mary. It's a name that I've always liked. Yet I think it's not as popular as it used to be. Do you like it?"

The question hung in the air for a time before she answered. "It's all right."

Mary Broughton, I thought.

Then I said, "Would you like to be called Mary?"

There was complete silence. My heart gave a leap. I had not intended to test her; it had simply slipped out.

At length she said, "Why do you ask?"

"Well, names are odd, aren't they? Some people are dissatisfied with the names they have and like to think of themselves as being called something else. When I was about ten I wanted to be called Roger and started writing Roger on the title page of books I owned. **This book belongs to Roger**. That sort of thing."

"You're not Roger," she said.

I laughed. "And you're not Mary."

She brought the conversation to an end. There was something on the cooker, she said, and she had the children's homework to correct.

"See you Friday evening," she said.

"Yes. I'm looking forward to that."

I WAS NERVOUS WHEN JENNY ARRIVED AT THE flat that Friday evening. I had spent several days thinking about our situation, and I had decided that I could not continue with a relationship that was affected by such a major issue of trust. I could have telephoned her and spoken about it, but I decided that it was just too difficult a subject to handle in anything but a face-to-face meeting. So I had made the decision to speak to her about it that Friday evening when we went out for dinner. I would tell her about how I had found Mary Broughton's passport and I would tell her exactly what Johnny had said to me in Paris. I would then raise the issue of Johnny's disappearance.

I hardly dared think about what I should do after that. Was it my duty to go to the police to tell them of my suspicions? And if I did go to them, should I just tell them about the finding of the passport, or should I bring in Johnny Bates too? If Johnny had been reported missing, then any information about what might have happened to him would surely have to be looked into. And yet one could not go around reporting people who one merely thought might have committed a crime; surely it had to be more concrete than that.

Jenny spotted my nervousness shortly after she came into the flat.

"Are you all right?"

"I'm fine."

She shook her head. "I don't think you are. You're jumpy."

I looked out of the window. We were standing in the kitchen, where I had just put a cafetière on the hot plate. She was standing behind me. I noticed that she was standing next to the knife block—one of those large blocks of wood with slits for the kitchen knives to be stored. My flatmate prided himself on his cooking knives, which were endorsed by some famous German chef. I glanced at the knives, and then out of the window again.

"Is Colin away for the whole weekend?" she asked.

I opened my mouth to answer, but something told me not to tell the truth. "Not this time," I said. "He might be back later this evening. I'm not sure what his plans are for tomorrow. I think there's a wedding out at Kew. Something like that." The wedding in question was due to take place the following Saturday, but I was frightened now and did not want her to think we would be on our own.

"You could have come out to my place," she said. "There's racing at Cheltenham. We could have gone."

I made some non-committal comment. I could not put the confrontation off any longer. I glanced at the knife block. Her hand was resting on it now. It would take just a flick of the wrist to get one of the knives out, and she was between me and the door . . .

"Could we talk?" I said. "Not in here. In the living room."

"Talk about what?"

"I'd just like to tell you what's worrying me."

She hesitated. My eye went to her hand on the knife block—it moved, but not towards the knives—away from them.

"Yes," she said. "I think we should."

She went into the living room before I did. I waited until the coffee was ready and then I poured us each a cup, topped it up with frothed milk, and then followed her.

"All right," she said, as she took the mug of coffee from me. "We can talk now. Are you having second thoughts?"

"About what?"

"About me. About us."

I saw my opening. "I'm afraid I am."

She was silent for a moment. She was gazing at me, not in any hostile way, but almost sadly. "I thought you were. You can always tell. You can tell when somebody falls out of love. It's like switching off a light. Click. Or maybe it's more like turning down a light that's on one of those dimmer switches—you know the sort—they make the light go down slowly until eventually it fades away altogether."

"A rheostat," I said.

"A what?"

"A rheostat gradually reduces the amount of power going to the bulb."

"Yes, like one of those."

I wondered if I could leave it like that. It would certainly be easier, but then it occurred to me that whatever my suspicions of Jenny might have been, I owed her an explanation.

"I found a passport in your room," I said. "It belonged to somebody called Mary Broughton."

She watched me.

"I looked at the back," I continued, "and I saw a couple of names—in your handwriting. One was Johnny Bates—the other one was . . . I forget who it was. But you had written it. And then when we were in Paris, Johnny said that you weren't called Jenny after all and that you were really somebody else altogether."

I paused. "Is that all?" she asked. "Is that what's been getting at you?"

"There's something more," I said. "Johnny Bates has gone missing. I spoke to somebody he shares a flat with, and he said that Johnny had disappeared."

She started to smile. I frowned. "I don't think this is at all funny," I said.

"Don't you? Well, I do. Do you want me to tell you why?"

I nodded.

"Mary Broughton is my cousin. She stayed with me for five weeks in the early spring. She left that passport in the house—she had a new one sent to her while she was with me and the Passport Office always returns the old one with the top clipped when you renew."

"And your handwriting?"

"I filled that in for her the previous year. We went to Spain together. I was filling in my person-to-be-informed details when we were at the airport and she handed me her passport and asked me to fill hers in for her. She didn't have a pen and she was in the middle of eating a burger—she had grease on her fingers."

I pondered this for a moment. There was an obvious flaw in her story.

"But why would she choose Johnny Bates as the person to be informed if she got into difficulty abroad?"

She hesitated for a moment. I noticed the hesitation; I was not imagining it. "Because she shared a flat with him and three others at the time. In Bristol."

"She shared with Johnny?"

"Yes. That's how I met him in the first place."

All I could say was "I see."

"So that explains all that," she said. "You should have asked me."

"And what about Johnny's disappearance?"

She shrugged. "He's done this before. Johnny goes walkabout. He comes back. But it's because he pushes off from time to time that he can't hold down a job. He's unstable. He's sweet underneath, but he's unstable."

"Are you worried about him?"

"No, not really. He'll come back and he'll forget about me eventually. As I said, it's the sort of thing he does."

I looked up at the ceiling. I suppose the predominant emotion I felt was embarrassment, but I also felt a sense of relief at having been proved wrong. It was just as well, I thought, that I had not gone to the police.

"Hugh?"

I had been thinking. "Sorry. Yes?"

"I said: Is that all that's worrying you? Is that why you've cooled towards me?"

I shrugged. "I suppose so. I feel a bit foolish. I thought . . ."

She rose from her chair and came over to envelop me in a hug. "Oh, my poor darling, you shouldn't have kept it to yourself. You should have talked to me. If something's bugging you, talk. You should always talk."

I felt like a child forgiven. "I will," I said.

"So let's go out to dinner—somewhere special. My treat."

"No. Mine."

She planted a kiss on my brow. "If you insist."

LATE THAT NIGHT, OR THE FOLLOWING morning—it might have been at two or three—I woke up. There was a full moon outside and the inadequate curtains in my room could not keep the room dark. I was lying on my back. I moved my arm gently under the sheet, expecting to feel Jenny lying beside me. I felt nothing.

I opened my eyes, very slowly, and saw that she was standing beside the bed on my side. She was looking down at me, although I could not make out her face, which was in shadow.

I held my breath. My stomach was a knot of fear; every muscle taut, and it was like that for something like twenty or thirty seconds. My instinct was to leap out of bed on the other side, but it occurred to me that if she had a knife she would still have the opportunity to use it before I escaped. Should I launch myself directly at her, using surprise? I might have a better chance that way.

But then Jenny suddenly moved away. She took a step back, turned and then walked round the end of the bed to her side. Then she slipped under the sheets, her back turned towards me. I heard her breathing; I heard her clear her throat quietly.

I lay absolutely still, and did not return to sleep for the remaining hours of the night. At seven o'clock I got up, had a shower and dressed. Then I went to my flatmate's desk in his room—I did not have my own desk—and took a sheet of his writing paper.

This isn't working, I wrote. **I'm so sorry. Please let yourself out. I'm very sorry about this and I hope that I haven't upset you too much. Hugh.**

I left the note on the kitchen table, where she would see it when she woke up. Then I left the flat, intending to come back at lunchtime, when I hoped the coast would be clear. There was no doubt in my mind that I had had a narrow escape.

"IS THAT THE END?" ASKED KAY. "YOU CAN'T leave us there."

"Not quite," said Hugh. "When I returned, I entered the flat tentatively, in case she was still there. But she had gone. There was a note for me on the table."

Dear Hugh, it read. **I understand how you must feel. I can explain things, but I don't think you're prepared to listen, and if you don't trust me then I see no point in our continuing our relationship. I've explained to you about Mary Broughton, and also about Johnny Bates. I suspect you don't believe me, but if you want to check up on what I said you can call Mary herself and ask her. I've written her number at the bottom of this note. As for Johnny, call his flat in a few days' time and see if he's back. I bet he will be.**

A final thing: I don't know if something happened last night. Maybe it did, and maybe that's why you've done this. I have something called a parasomnia. It means that I can do things at night—like thrashing about or even walking in my sleep. I know that can make people nervous, but there's not much I can do about it, I'm afraid.

I went to a sleep clinic in Bristol, and they said that it's more common than people imagine. But they also suggested that I should speak to any partners about it—and I should have spoken to you. The truth is that I'm a bit ashamed of it. All I do in the somnambulistic state is walk around the room. Sometimes I open cupboards and then close them. That's what most somnambulists do—nothing meaningful. But you don't trust me anyway, so there's no need for us to go into that any further. I hope things work out well for you. Love, Jenny.

"Oh my God!" said David. "What a tricky situation. What did you do?"

"What do you think I should have done?"

"Kept well away," said Kay. "And I wouldn't trust her, frankly. Somnambulism? I wonder . . ."

Andrew shook his head. "She's innocent," he said.

"I'm not sure I would have taken the risk," said David. "But one thing interests me: Did Johnny Bates turn up again?"

"Yes. He reappeared."

"What did he say?" asked Andrew.

"I phoned him again. He was very uncommunicative."

"So she hadn't disposed of him?"

"Obviously not."

"And Mary Broughton?" asked David.

"I met her. She existed. She confirmed that everything Jenny had said was true."

They looked at one another.

"We have to trust people," said Hugh. "And not every love affair is **absolutely** safe, is it?"

They looked at one another again.

"I'm seeing her again," he continued. "We're going back to Paris."

David cleared his throat, and the others looked at him expectantly. But he did not speak for a while. He just looked doubtful. Then he said, "I see."

"Should you?" ventured Kay.

"Trust," said Hugh. "As I said, we have to trust others."

"Wouldn't it be better to . . . to meet somebody else?" This from David.

"But perhaps not on a railway platform," suggested Andrew.

"Did you see **Brief Encounter**?" asked David. "Celia Johnson. It takes place in a railway station. It's one of the great romantic films of all time. Black and white, of course. I always find black and white more romantic."

"No," said Hugh. "I never saw it."

"Perhaps you should."

David was thinking of black and white; of flickering images. "Nothing's ever really black and white, is it?" he said.

Andrew was frowning. "The photograph," he said. "Why was the photograph removed from the passport?"

At first Hugh said nothing. He looked out of the

train window, over fields stretching out into deep England; there were quiet lanes leading into the green heart of flat country; there were distant cooling towers from which white clouds of steam arose. Would that come down as rain? Would it?

Then Hugh cleared his throat. "Oh," he said.

35

"I WAS FIVE," SAID KAY, "WHEN MY BROTHER was born. Like me, he was born in Adelaide. I went down with my mother about four weeks before he was due and there was one point on the train when we thought things might be starting. I was excited: it would have been wonderful, I thought, to have a baby brother born on a train, and they told me I was bitterly disappointed when it did not happen."

My father was overjoyed. His son was called Stewart, which had been the name of his own father back in Scotland. He was a bright-eyed little boy, with his father's fair hair. I shared my father's pride in him. I wrote stories for him and laughed at his antics. As he grew older, he looked up to me more and more, joining me in the games I played with imaginary friends—there were no other children for many miles and we made up by inventing them. I had a friend called Jessie, who was good at finding things and had a cat called Frankie. He conjured up a boy called Danny who was immensely strong and had a small red aeroplane. We believed in them and spent long hours in their company.

My mother watched all this bemused. "What does Frankie like to eat?" she asked.

"Sardines," I answered. "Sardines and sometimes Vegemite sandwiches."

"And does Frankie catch mice?"

"No, Frankie catches kangaroos. He's the only cat in Australia who can catch a full-size kangaroo. He's very strong."

"And Danny's aeroplane—where does he keep it?"

"He keeps it in Sydney when he doesn't need it. It flies here by itself when he calls it."

We had a wonderful childhood in that place, so far from everything else. Schooling was by radio—we followed the school of the air and I still remember those hot mornings, sitting around the radio transmitter, the generator thumping away in the background, listening to our teacher call the roll and be answered by children from hundreds of miles away.

Then, when I was ten and my brother was five I was sent off to boarding school in Adelaide. This was a place run by nuns, and I was terrified. I had heard that nuns could be strict and that if you misbehaved they hit you with a ruler on the back of your knees. Not all nuns are like that, of course. I know there are plenty who are kind and gentle but these ones, I'm afraid, were not. One day I shall pluck up the courage to go back to that school and confront the past. There are no nuns left there, I'm told, and the school is run by lay-teachers. But I need to make that journey before I can lay my education to rest.

My brother stayed at the siding. I wrote to him sometimes from the school boardinghouse and told him about some of the nuns. **I hate them. I hope that this place burns down one day and I can come back to Hope Springs and see you again. Jessie is here and she hates it too. Frankie is with her and he's going to get even with the nuns one day. Cats are good at that, you know. Those nuns should look out, the cows. Love from your sister.**

One of my letters was intercepted by the nun in charge of the boardinghouse. She called me to her study and said, "You are a wicked child, and you have let Jesus and the Holy Virgin down. You've let them down very badly." She then hit me with her ruler and told me to go to confession and tell the priest about how I had written wicked things in a letter. "And may God forgive you," she added. "Because I won't be doing so in a hurry."

SHORTLY BEFORE MY BROTHER'S SEVENTH birthday he was bitten by a king brown snake. He was playing near the water tower—a favourite place of his—and he lifted up an old wooden box that somebody had left at the base of the structure. The snake was underneath the box and it bit him on the wrist. Unfortunately, a fang penetrated the veins that run there and so the venom was very quickly carried through his system.

My father heard his cries and came to the scene very quickly. The snake had moved, but he was able to identify it. He knew how serious it was and he immediately went on the radio to the Flying Doctor service in Port Augusta. They promised that they would come up right away and that the best thing would be for him to get Stewart to the nearest town. There was a nurse there who could administer serum and they would then get him to hospital.

He and my mother started the car, but at that point Stewart was already very badly affected. They contacted the Flying Doctor again, and they revised their advice. They should keep him immobile if possible and not subject him to the car journey. Their plane would be taking off in a matter of minutes.

Stewart died forty minutes after the bite. It was unusual for a bite from that type of snake to be lethal quite so quickly, but they thought that the snake had injected a particularly large amount of venom. They also said that because Stewart was so young the effect of the bite was more dramatic.

He was already buried when I came up from Adelaide on the next train. His grave was by a stand of eucalyptus trees, a small mound on which flowers had been laid. These were flowers from the beds that my mother had tended so carefully. She could not have imagined that the flowers she nursed would be on the grave of her child.

THEY STAYED AT HOPE SPRINGS IN SPITE OF the tragedy. My father became depressed, I was told later, and had to be sent off to hospital in Adelaide for four months. He was grieving for his son, of course. While he was away in hospital, my mother ran the siding. She continued to cultivate her flowers, she continued to bake the scones that she sold to passengers on their way to Alice, she still kept the house spotless. She did everything, as such women did. They never complained. They did everything.

I had become too old for imaginary friends, but somehow I felt that I should keep Danny going. I made a small place for him on a windowsill where he could land his red aeroplane and I sometimes left a glass of lemonade there for him to drink before he took off in his plane. Ants would discover it and crawl up the side of the glass, delighted at the find of sugary drink.

"Why is there lemonade on the window?" my mother asked. "It'll just attract those ants."

"It's there for Danny."

She looked away. Children, being naturally optimistic and cheerful, cannot begin to guess at the sadness of the adult heart.

In due course they took me out of the convent school and sent me to a government school, also in Adelaide. I did well there, away from the nuns, and ended up going to the University of Western Australia in Perth. I met my husband there. He's a geologist. He couldn't come on this trip to Scotland because he was sent up to a place near Broome for three months and he wanted me to treat myself to something while he was up there.

I think of my parents and Hope Springs. They are both dead now—they retired to Perth so that they could be near me. They had a short retirement—life works out like that for some people. They work hard all their lives and then their health doesn't hold out for long once they retire. They would never have complained about that, because complaining was not part of their nature.

I went back to Hope Springs a few years ago—I wanted to show my husband what it was like. The railway line was moved and the Ghan now follows a different route to Alice Springs, and Darwin, too, of course. But the siding is still there because things remain in the dry climate of the Outback. Things don't rot out there—the ants may get them, the red earth may cover them, they may get blown away, but they don't really rot.

The station-master's house is there. It still has its roof although there are no doors. I found my room—there it was, and there was the windowsill on which I had left the glass of lemonade for Danny.

And outside, near the trees, was the mound of my brother's grave. The edges of it had softened with the action of the wind, but it was still recognisable as a child's grave.

My husband held my hand. I wept.

Then, going back to the house, he said, "They must have loved one another a lot, your parents. For your mother to come out here—all the way from Sydney—and live this lonely, lonely life. They must have loved one another very deeply."

"They did," I said.

And I thought of the life they had led. I loved them very much, you see, my father and my mother, who didn't ever get anywhere very much or achieve great things. Other than a well-kept station and some flowers in the desert. Is that enough? I like to think that it is.

37

OF COURSE IT IS, THOUGHT DAVID. OF course it is. And now the London station—King's Cross; into darkness first and then above them, high and silver-grey, the glass sky that arches over the platforms—a whole scurrying world. He smiled goodbye to Andrew and Hugh and to Kay, these people whom he would never see again. And they smiled back and they shook hands, surprised, touched by the intimacy of the conversation, and by the lives laid bare. Kay thought: Each of us has his or her reasons, for making this journey, for being as we are, for continuing with the lives we lead; ordinary lives, of course, but touched here and there with moments of understanding and insight, and sheer marvel. She reached up for her bag from the shelf above the seats, but Andrew had already done that for her and gave it to her, and she thanked him without saying anything; one can do that, one can thank another with one's eyes, one's hands, with any of a thousand gestures.

She moved towards the door. She stopped. Loving others, she thought, is the good thing we do in our lives.

About the Author

Alexander McCall Smith is the author of the No. 1 Ladies' Detective Agency series, the Isabel Dalhousie series, the Portuguese Irregular Verbs series, the 44 Scotland Street series, and the Corduroy Mansions series. He is professor emeritus of medical law at the University of Edinburgh and has served with many national and international organizations concerned with bioethics. He was born in what is now known as Zimbabwe and taught law at the University of Botswana. He lives in Scotland.